America, of Thee I Sing

By

John R. Stanczak

To My friends,
Larry & JoAnn

Enjoy the book
as much as I enjoyed
writing it.

John R. Stanczak

Acknowledgements

This venture would not have been as enjoyable as it was if not for the enormous amount of expert help that I received from my two co-contributors. Their ever-present willingness to help with every aspect of this venture, and their untiring dedication to the project, merits my utmost appreciation. From the tedious and monotonous task of editing, formatting, and creating the book's cover, their prints were all over the final outcome. I truly offer my sincere appreciation to Hannah and Jordan Turner for all that they offered. It's a blessing to have their family as neighbors and as ever-present help when needed.

I have no doubt that this book would not have been completed without their extensive help.

Table of Contents

Chapter 1: Nature's Fireworks

Chapter 2: Troubling Events

Chapter 3: A Harrowing Trip to the Fairgrounds

Chapter 4: A Welcome and Charitable Stranger

Chapter 5: Unwelcome Company

Chapter 6: Remorseful Reminiscing

Chapter 7: And They're Off and Running

Chapter 8: Post Race Complications

Chapter 9: Rose's Dilemma

Chapter 10: A Call to Action

Chapter 11: Venturing Out

Chapter 12: An Unheeded Warning

Chapter 13: The Great Escape

Chapter 14: Parting Brings Much Sorrow

Chapter 15: A Compassionate Trade

Chapter 16: Continued Threats

Chapter 17: Much to Be Thankful For

Chapter 18: Seeking Safe Harbor

Chapter 19: Justice Is Swift and Fair

Chapter 20: Depression Demands

Chapter 21: On the Road Again

Chapter 22: A Foiled Plan

Chapter 23: Wartime Service

Chapter 24: Winter Woes

Chapter 25: Lives Well Lived

"It was like a kaleidoscope in print leading one on all the twists and turns in the story. I found it to be reminiscent of the families whose dedication to each other sparks the determination to achieve success. The warmth of the saga made it very easy to connect with all of the characters.

Only America offers this unique opportunity to improve your station in life."

- Joseph P.

America, of Thee I Sing

Chapter 1:
Nature's Fireworks

It was Saturday evening in early 1929, at the Barrow's homestead, and as usual, the family had gathered after dinner to engage in a friendly game of cards. The weather outside made it an excellent place to be, as a ferocious wind blew the falling rain violently up against the windows and blinded the sight to the outside. It made it impossible to see whether any farm animals were distressed. It was an uncomfortable situation for Elmo, who resided with his only son Zack, the head of the household. Elmo was concerned about the mare who was near giving birth to the first colt to be born on Happy Acres Farm.

The farm in Webster County, rural Mississippi, was the site of a fierce battle against Indian tribes in 1770. It was a battle that saw the Choctaws and the Chickasaws exterminate the powerful Chocchuma tribe. It was a peaceful county with the county seat located in the city of Walthall, boasting a population of 12,644 according to the 1920 census. It was anything but quiet this evening as the raging storm supplied plenty of fireworks, with fiery lightning flashes followed by crashing claps of thunder. The combination of both led to an unnerving chain of events that evening.

Meanwhile, Elmo seriously engaged the family in their favorite pastime in the comfort of the warmth afforded by a fireplace with sparks and embers raining down like winter snow. It was a card game that had garnered the name "Grandpa's Game." It probably derived its name from the fact that Grandpa Elmo was most generally the winner of the games. Granddaughters, Rose, and Camelia would affirm that he was a winner in whatever he endeavored to do. His only other grandchild, Robbie, found him to be his hero and tried to emulate him throughout his lifetime. He certainly deserved whatever accolades were heaped upon him as far as Zack and Zack's wife, Tessie, were concerned.

Their family was very atypical of all of the neighboring folks. They were hard-working people who primarily derived their income from working on the land, engaging in raising livestock, or planting crops. It was not an easy life, and the income earned from their hard work was meager. A saving grace for their family was the fact that they all worked in harmony, with the common good of all being the driving force behind their activities. Zack worked at a neighboring farm to earn extra income. At the same time, Elmo performed most of the needed tasks associated with maintaining the property and tending to the livestock. Robbie, who had just entered high school, was quite capable of tending to the crops in the fields. He would come home after school and tend to the necessary chores, and in his later school years, would apply all of his efforts and time to these tasks while on summer vacation. Rose, the eldest daughter, had her sight set on going to college after completing her senior year and devoted her time to filling in for her mother, who worked at the local high school as a cafeteria worker. She aspired to become a nurse and took measures to learn all she could about the profession before getting her formal education. Tessie's position allowed her to start early in the morning and be home before Rose, Robbie, and Camelia returned. Camelia, the middle child, was in her sophomore year at high school and was still undecided about what she might choose as a profession. Her immediate choices were between teaching grade school and becoming an accountant. She became the dish and pot washer in the family. Robbie, at this time, was resigned to continue to work on the family farm. His primary interest in doing so lay in the fact that he was a Hippophile, a genuinely devoted lover of everything equestrian-related.

Their devotion to each other was necessary if everyone's wishes and dreams were to become a reality. The current economic situation was not exactly sympathetic to their aspirations, and the family was aware of this. It was evident that Elmo could not perform his duties consistently. Zack's temporary employment could be terminated at any time. Tessie's employment offered the most security at this time but provided the lowest income. They were all aware that the loss of Zack's job was the biggest threat to their dreams being fulfilled.

The card game was in full swing, with Camelia and Grandpa in the best position to be declared the winner. Camelia was generally the one who most challenged Grandpa's desire to be number one. He loved to win. Rose dealt out the cards for the last hand of the game, and it appeared that either one of the two was most likely to emerge triumphant. As they gathered their cards to continue the game, a deafening thunder rocked the night, adding to the night's violence. It was followed by what appeared to be another close lightning strike. It was evident that this game would not be completed right now. Elmo, Zack, and Robbie immediately knew from the peal of the thunder and the brilliant light emitted from the lightning strike that all the commotion could certainly spook the animals. They proceeded to hurry over to the barn area to determine the effect of the storm on the animals. Their first thought was that some of the animals needed help. Thankfully, there was no sign that the lightning strike caused a fire, and they found great relief knowing that was the case.

Upon further exploration, it became apparent that our mare, Sally, was in distress from labor pain. Elmo, who had been present at several normal births where the mare had reached the standard gestation period of 320 to 380 days, was concerned that Sally was at day 301. He was aware that most mares foal at night, and from noticing that her teats had distended along with signs of red bag, he felt there was no time left to call a vet. Sally was becoming increasingly anxious, the foal was starting to kick, and Sally was now in a heavy sweat. These were all signs that another member of the animal population would soon be coming into the world.

There was little time to waste. Sally required immediate attention. Elmo hurriedly sprang into action. He wrapped the mare's tail and cleaned the perineal section. Now was the time for Sally to do her part, and it was not long before fluid came rushing out. Everything was going ahead in perfect order, and about 15 minutes later, the front hooves and nose presented themselves in a caudal fashion. Elmo moved to guide the rest of the foal out, and upon full presentation, started to wipe the newborn down. Within an hour, a beautiful colt lifted himself onto weak, spindly legs. Elmo performed all of the necessary after-birth precautions, and he administered an enema to evacuate the meconium. The miracle of birth that Elmo performed this night was as if an experienced veterinarian had competently worked his magic.

All that transpired on this eventful stormy evening left Elmo grateful that he could help deliver this beautiful young colt, aptly named Sparky, due to the pyrotechnics that nature had provided. He took his part in the birthing process very matter-of-factly and was mystified as to how all of the necessary medical supplies were on hand to do so. Robbie, who aspired to be a horse breeder, had read a medical journal outlining the procedure. It prompted him to be prepared for an emergency that probably saved two lives. Robbie learned a great deal that day, much of which would benefit him in his later life.

They were both exhausted from the experience and wondered how Zack had made out tending to the other animals. He quickly responded that all was in order and that none of the other animals seemed to show any signs of anguish from the night's proceedings. Grandpa wanted to get back to the house to finish the card game. Robbie was exhausted but acquiesced to Grandpa's request to continue with the game and the others were all in to do so in order to please Grandpa. It was a bit easier to accept continuing on, because it was the last hand in the game. The final hand seemed to take an eternity to complete since it presented the biggest challenge to the players. It was a tranquil game that proceeded, and neither contender showed any signs of confidence that they would emerge triumphant. After about 45 minutes of playing, it appeared that a dark horse would ultimately be declared the winner. Tessie beat out the two aspirants but did not show any signs of exuberance, so as not to deflate Grandpa this evening. He was down in the dumps obsessed over his unlucky loss. He knew he had been too tired to play cards considering the ordeal he had been through. Before everyone retired for the evening, they made it a point to extend appreciation to Grandpa and Robbie for a job well done.

Zack emphasized that it was a good night and that there was no property damage. Two animals were most likely alive due to their heroics, and all other farm animals seemed content. He also pointed out that Sparky was eagerly suckling on Sally's teats. All was good at the Barrows at this time.

Chapter 2:
Troubling Events

A new day was dawning, and the family awakened to a Monday that offered bright sunshine, soft southern winds, and a mild temperature. The sun glanced off the small farm pond and seemed to dance as the wind softly caused the water to ripple. It reflected off the kitchen ceiling alternately featuring various hues and brought a soothing feeling of contentment to the breakfast diners. Rose's fine cooking would soon offer further delight to all. Tessie had already left for work at the school cafeteria, and Rose was substituting for her in her absence. The family was in for a meal that would have their taste buds yearning for more. Her menu for the day featured scrambled eggs with cheese mixed in, biscuits, country ham, and hash-brown potatoes. The diners all agreed that she had done a fantastic job and ate as if they meant what they said. It was proof that actions speak louder than words. A bit of small talk took place as they finished dining, and the diners disclosed what the day had in store for them one by one.

There were only two weeks left in the school year, and soon the children would all be off doing whatever was necessary. Rose was concerned about the chemistry test scheduled for today. Her last test earned a grade of ninety-two, and she was not happy with the results. Today, she felt that she had to have a perfect score to qualify for the Science Scholarship Award that her teacher, Mr. Spengler, sought to award her. Younger sister, Camelia, was always on edge when going to school because of the actions of a particular girl, Callie, who continually tormented her. Robbie hoped Sally would not act up on the way to school today. His last ride on her was disconcerting due to her strange and unusual behavior. He wanted this school year to end so that he could spend precious time with Sparky. Papa Zack was excited and happy to have them home for the summer to lend more help with chores. Grandpa was delighted that they would be more available for him to love and to be able to pass on to Robbie some of the knowledge he gained in his early years in rural Kentucky.

Rose and Camelia were off to school riding with their neighbor's dad in his old Ford auto. Robbie tried to saddle Sally, who had been very mild and relaxed up to this point, but she did not accept his attempt to do so. While inspecting the saddle, it became apparent that somebody had glued a small piece of jute rope on the underside, causing Sally discomfort. He removed the rope and placed the saddle back onto Sally with no objection to his doing so. He mounted up and proceeded on toward school. On the way, he pondered who might do such a thing and why. He reflected on a recent incident where he found the bedding fork with the tines facing upwards lying in Sparky's stall. He was sure that neither Grandpa nor Dad would have allowed that to happen. These two incidents occurring so close within one another were very unnerving to him. There would be no learning for him at school today, as his mind was fixated on "who" and "why."

The girls arrived at school, and as they walked up to the entrance, Camelia informed Rose that Callie was pointing at her as she talked with several other girls. Rose cautioned Camelia not to respond or react in any manner, to whatever else Callie confronted her with today. Robbie arrived, removed the saddle, and led Sally to the lean-to in order to protect her from the grueling sun. He nuzzled her and affectionately slapped her on her hindquarter. Robbie glanced back at Sally and slowly sauntered off to class. His last thought was that he did not want to leave her on this day.

The school day ended with some real positives. Rose was confident that she did well on her test when her teacher, Mr. Spengler, smiled at her after having time to review the test paper she had turned in to him. Camelia was happy after receiving an apology from Callie, who asked if they might become friends. Rose intercepted Callie as they were in route to the cafeteria for lunch and admonished her for her treatment of Camelia. She advised her that if it continued, it would hurt her mother's sewing business because several of her friend's mothers might find it necessary to seek help elsewhere. Callie responded remorsefully, professing that she was sorry and had no intentions of continuing her bad behavior. Camelia, who felt a confrontation was necessary to achieve this goal, was delighted with her sister's results. She also agreed that a better ending comes when conflict is not the answer to a problem. The solution was the reaction of a reasonable person responding to sound advice from good parents. Robbie was happy that no harm fell to Sally, but he completed the homeward-bound trip in high alert mode. The recent events left him in a state of concern.

Robbie wasted no time after arriving home to seek out Grandpa Elmo to ask him a few questions that might help clarify things. When he brought up the careless placement of the bedding fork, Grandpa assured him that he would never let that happen, nor would his father. Robbie also explained the situation of the jute rope glued to the underside of the saddle and the effect it had on Sally. Elmo suggested it could have had something to do with a young lad named Rolf who was at the farm last Wednesday in the early evening. This was the same lad that came to look at Sparky previously. Grandpa recalled him saying that Robbie would be there to talk to him. Robbie remembered Rolf asking him what he would be doing that day and had informed him that he was going to dinner with a church group early in the evening. He also told Rolf that Grandpa and his dad would probably not be home either because they were considering buying another horse. Rolf was keenly interested in Sparky and Sally and had asked many questions about their lineage.

This did not sit well with Robbie, and he told Grandpa he would do some sleuth work. Grandpa told Robbie he needed other eyes and ears on the case and that he was the man for the job. Even Sherlock Holmes needed the help of Dr. Watson to solve his mysteries. Robbie quickly accepted his offer and told "Watson" he was on the job. He wondered if all this was related to the upcoming horse race that would take place at the Fourth of July celebration at the Fairgrounds. The concern for the safety of the horses became of vital importance. It reasoned that the stable would have to be closely guarded, which would be hard to do when a person was out in the field or went into town for supplies or other purposes.

Grandpa's answer to guarding the stable was simple but had never been employed because of the concern for the disturbance it might create. Their farm dog, Rollo, was a good guard dog. He would be able to alert them to any activity that was out of the norm but had always been penned up for fear of what he might do in an encounter with someone. The decision to place him, untied, inside the stable was made with some concern.

Fears of a disturbance came about the first two nights Rollo was in the stable. He responded with his booming bark to every new sound the stable environment offered, as they were all strange to him. He had to learn to recognize and differentiate unintimidating sounds from those that signaled danger.

Chapter 3:
A Harrowing Trip to the Fairgrounds

Summer vacation arrived, and it came none too soon, as the temperatures had reached the 90-degree mark so early in the season. This type of weather would have made it unbearable to be in class. The freedom from the classroom routine was greatly welcomed by all. The family day began early in the morning, and with breakfast behind them, they were all about doing chores that were part of their daily routine. Camelia was busy cleaning the kitchen and the breakfast dishes everyone had emptied and enjoyed. Rose, having already been occupied with cooking, was now set about to tidy up the house. She was soon to be joined by Camelia. Grandpa was busy repairing a section of fence that needed some mending. Robbie had not started to work yet, as he was enjoying some familiarization time with Sparky. This was a necessary time that allowed them to become trusting in each other. It was certainly also a time from which Robbie derived great pleasure, and that Sparky wanted more of. Although not all the family were together at this time of the day, it was a time enjoyed by those present.

The sun shined, ever so beautifully, and grew more intense as time passed. It would soon cause some concern for anybody working out of doors. It was bearable, but it certainly was uncomfortable and would take its toll on a person after some time. Being aware of the conditions, Rose took it upon herself to make a pitcher of lemonade and took it to Elmo and Robbie. They both confessed that the lemonade was deliciously refreshing and enjoyed the brief respite from their chores. Rose cautioned Grandpa to be aware of the heat to avoid a possible heat stroke.

The noon hour found them all gathered at the table, joined by Tessie, to have lunch. Due to the heat, the ladies did not fuss much and prepared a relaxed, light lunch. Other than asking Tessie about her day, the conversation was sparse, and soon everyone left to resume their day's work. As Grandpa left, he requested Robbie join him, as the fence-mending job was more than he bargained for.

Robbie was reluctant to lose sight of the stable area but honored the request to join Elmo and gathered what he felt might be necessary extra tools for the job. He joined in and at once went to work stretching the wire that Grandpa had spread out on the ground to be attached to the poles. After some time, Robbie noticed that Grandpa favored his right hand, and he inquired about the problem. Grandpa said it was nothing serious and ended the conversation. Robbie did not feel that was the case and insisted on looking at his hand. It was evident that Grandpa was injured more seriously than he had wanted Robbie to believe. He had a terrible bruise featuring black, blue, red, and purple tones. Seeing it convinced Robbie that Grandpa's work had ended for the day. Robbie persuaded him to return to the house and get ready to leave for the doctor's office while he picked up the tools and put them away. He spent a few minutes checking on Sally and Sparky and hurried to the house. Robbie called for his mother, who was busy in the kitchen, and wondered what she thought about Grandpa's injury. Tessie was unaware of his injury and said that Elmo had gone to his room after spending time in the bathroom without mentioning anything to her.

Grandpa was quiet on the way to the doctor's office and showed no signs of extreme pain. He waited for Tessie to open the car door for him, and then they all went into the office together. It was not long before Nurse Jane ushered them into the exam room. Grandpa insisted that there was no need for him to be there. After a few minutes, Dr. Gil Morgan entered the room. Dr. Morgan was the only doctor in the town of Europa and had been practicing for over thirty years. He was considered an excellent doctor, and as a general practitioner, was capable of handling most situations with which he was presented. He had no intentions of retiring soon, and for a man of fifty-eight years of age, appeared to be and acted much younger.

He asked Elmo if he was in pain, to which Elmo replied that he had some. At a brief glance, he suspected Elmo was in more than just a little pain. After a thorough examination, Dr. Morgan found Elmo suffering from a severe thumb sprain involving the ulnar collateral ligament, possibly making his thumb feel unstable. He told Elmo that he would splint his thumb to see if that would allow for proper healing. He would see him back in a week to decide if a cast would have to replace the splint to attain the desired results. Dr. Morgan told him this was a severe injury and must be considered as such and cared for properly. His departing orders were to refrain from all work requiring hand use for a month. A somber Elmo left the office of his friend and doctor with a reminder to return in a week for the follow-up visit.

It was late when they arrived home, and Elmo felt slightly muddled from the injection he received to help quell the pain. The two girls were overly concerned when they saw their loving Grandpa with a thumb splint applied to his hand. They offered words of sympathy to him, which he felt was unnecessary because he would be fine by next week. They all hoped that would be the case but cautioned him over his optimism. Zack did not show the deep concern that he was feeling over the incident and its impending complications. It was time for all to retire for the evening.

One by one, they entered the kitchen on another bright sunny day but seemed to have a heavy cloud hanging over their heads. There was no time for doom and gloom, and hopefully, no real reason. Robbie finished his breakfast hurriedly, shoved his plate away, and began to offer words of encouragement to everybody. He professed that he was up to the task of picking up Grandpa's part of the workload. With that said, he gulped down the rest of his coffee and left without his usual second cup of joe. Rose emitted a smile of confidence and carried on with her routine. Camelia called out to Robbie to inform him that she was capable of helping with his now double load.

It was mid-morning, a much more pleasant day weather-wise, and Robbie had completed the fence mending that was left undone. He was pretty pleased with how it turned out and proud of the fact that he was able to carry out the task by himself. It crossed his mind that Grandpa would be mighty proud of him right now. It seemed like only seconds had passed when Robbie looked back over his shoulder and saw his idol flashing a smile that stretched from ear to ear. Grandpa credited him for his excellent work and wished he could have done such a fine job. Elmo told Robbie that the girls would be serving lunch within the hour. Robbie nodded and said he would be ready to eat a big lunch. After checking on the horses, lunch was his immediate priority. All was well at the stables, and Sally and Sparky were glad to see their buddy. Robbie wanted to spend more time with them and vowed to do so.

The lunch waiting for Robbie was an offering that he could not delay another minute. It was as if a magnetic force was compelling him inside. He hurried into the house and promptly seated himself at the kitchen table. Rose felt aware of his eagerness to indulge and quickly set a plate of food she had prepared in front of him. He tossed her a smile of approval and began to eat. The family members were surprised at his actions because he would never start to eat before everyone else was seated and all the diners had taken the time to offer sincere thanks for the meal.

Grandpa asked him if he was hungry or just in a hurry. Robbie realized that the question directed at him was due to his unusual behavior and apologized for his actions. He replied that he was in fact hungry, and yes, in a hurry. The reason for being so was due to his schedule's added work and wanting to spend more time with the horses. The annual Fourth of July race at the fairgrounds was looming over his shoulders and he needed to get Sally over to the fairgrounds to do some training. He had not been riding her as much as he should in preparation for the race and she still needed to build her endurance. Robbie also needed to regain that familiarity that had been absent lately to restore his confidence. That would happen if he got in more saddle time and if Sally and him were together more often. Dr. Sloan said she was healthy and ready for the race, and Zack had already paid the entry fee.

The afternoon found Grandpa and Robbie in the stable. They engaged in conversation regarding race preparations as Robbie freshened up the horses' stalls. The neighing of the horses was music to Robbie's ears and made him aware of the pleasure he got from just being there with them. Sparky also seemed pleased with his attention. It was clear that he was getting taller and had complete balance control. All signs indicated his conformation was progressing, as he exhibited excellent muscle development and fine structure. Sparky's soft snorts assured Elmo that he and Robbie were totally comfortable and close to each other.

The plans for today were in full swing, and Robbie stood for a moment to watch the beauty of the sunrise. Soft rays of sunlight filtered over the horizon, allowing him to proceed with fastening the horse trailer to the tractor. Zack's friend specially built the trailer in repayment for work he had performed for him after a strong spring wind had blown the roof off of his house. It was enclosed and featured insulated walls, ample headroom, a heavy hardwood floor, and extra width, allowing for side-to-side movement. His friend had certainly repaid his favor by building a safe and secure horse trailer.

Sally quickly loaded onto the trailer, and Robbie got behind the wheel and proceeded down the drive to turn onto the main road. A left turn would take them toward town and a right turn towards the Fairgrounds. The road to the Fairground was lightly traveled, and the tractor's slow speed would not hinder other traffic. En route, a black car with a distinctive-looking hood ornament came speeding dangerously close to the tractor and trailer. Robbie's evasive action caused the trailer to sway dangerously. Since they were traveling at a slow speed, Robbie managed to get the trailer back under control quickly. The car was the same one that Grandpa told Robbie he had noticed traveling by the farm often. A shaken and concerned Robbie promptly checked to ensure that Sally was alright. This incident proved to him that someone was trying to cause harm. He was thankful for the stability of the Fordson tractor.

Concerned about the safety of Sally and the equipment, the unloading, exercising, and reloading was completed with a wary eye. The time at the Fairgrounds was rewarding, and the horse and rider profited from the stimulating session. Sally performed beautifully. Without exerting herself, she exhibited the long fluid stride that Standardbreds possess. The exercise convinced Robbie that her endurance was strong and of no concern. Allowing Sally to run free in the pasture was good judgement and served her well. He felt confident that a definite bond existed that allowed Sally and him to be in perfect sync. The upcoming workouts would focus on her ability to get off to a fast start. He cautiously returned to the farm while wondering what might happen next.

The July Fourth race contenders arrived home safely. Sally was rubbed down and returned to her stall, and Robbie was off to fill his dad and grandfather in on today's disconcerting incident. Upon hearing the story, Zack was angered and worried by what happened. He recommended that Robbie be very alert and inform him of any future misadventures. Grandpa confessed that he was glad it was the tractor and not the pickup truck pulling the trailer.

The acquisition of the tractor had initially presented a double-edged sword to the family. Grandpa strongly resisted the deal because he knew much more about curing an ailing horse than about the repairing of a new-fangled contraption. He objected so strongly because he also had to sell his beloved Smoky in exchange for it. The future would prove this was ultimately a good trade.

Chapter 4:
A Welcome and Charitable Stranger

It was in October of 1928 that the impressive Colonel Robert Burns entered the picture in the serene town of Europa. The serenity and natural beauty of the area were very appealing and immediately attracted his interest. He set about to find a large parcel of land upon which he built his retirement. The spring fed pond on the property, and the beautiful Southern Live Oak and Black Gum trees that shaded it, were certainly factors that were added inducements in his purchase decision. The house that graced the picturesque property was modest in size but featured every creature comfort available to man. Because of the years he spent in the service of his country as a cavalry officer, and his innate love for horses, it was inevitable that a well-equipped horse barn would also be built to shelter the horses he would set out to buy. Apparently, the decision to settle here, rather than in an affluent locale noted for equine activities, best suited him for what he needed for fulfillment in his later life.

Colonel Burns was sometimes addressed as "Colonel," "Bob" by a few, and "That Man" by those who may have seen him from a distance or may have never seen him. The latter term resulted from the generosity that was so often shown by him. He was a gentleman farmer living among many neighboring farmers whose lives were vastly different from his own. His father and mother were principals in a Boston brokerage firm, and as a result, he was never deprived of anything in his youth. Early on, the farming in Europa was simply something to occupy him and to escape boredom. As time went on the chore took on more significance and became a pleasure to him. The pleasure was not so much from the toil, but rather from what he was doing with the fruits of his labor.

The Colonel would drive up his unneeded flatbed trailer to the front of his drive and load it with all varieties of vegetables that he was raising at the time. A large sign that stood next to the trailer displayed the message:

"IF YOU ARE NEEDY, TAKE ALL THAT YOU NEED, AND ONLY THAT WHICH YOU WILL NOT WASTE."

Word of this activity filtered throughout the county and attracted a good many people. It was of extreme pleasure for him to continue this practice during uncertain economic times. He felt good about what he was doing; however, the sight of the people who were so severely affected by the economic conditions of the time proved to be heartbreaking to him. These were the ones that affectionately referred to him as "That Man."

His enlistment in the Army came shortly after the end of his senior year at Boston College, where he graduated Magna Cum Laude. His parents decried his decision to do so, but he was intent on joining the Army. His time spent at school endeared him to the camaraderie in which he found so much enjoyment. This, coupled with his love of horses, offered him the opportunity to do what he found necessary to provide a feeling of contentment in his life.

It was no accident that he chose to join the cavalry upon his enlistment into the Army. He was an experienced horseman and had been engaged in equine activities all his life. He took part in steeplechase racing at an early age and continued at Boston College. He had finished first in many of his endeavors during that time and was a celebrated horseman. The stable behind his parent's well-appointed home was replete with some outstanding equine athletes. Young Robert was no stranger to any one of the horses and spent many hours in the saddle cantering at a leisurely pace or galloping wildly through the estate.

Shortly after the completion of his home in Europa, the urge to ride compelled him to seek out a reputable horse breeder and purchase his first horse. After much searching and seeking advice regarding potential horse dealers, he was directed to the folks over at Happy Acres Farm. At first glance he was not impressed with the property, nor the stable. However, it did not take long for him to realize that he was dealing with two men who possessed both integrity and tremendous knowledge about horses. After a prolonged conversation, Elmo and Zack showcased the horses that were on the selling block. The horses were paraded before the Colonel, but none of them seemed to pique his interest or whet his appetite. Elmo and Zack recognized his interest in a stallion bearing the name Smoky, who was named for his distinct coloration. The dappled gray that was lightly blended into his midnight black color added to Colonel Bob's admiration for the well conformed animal. Unfortunately, Smoky was not on the selling block.

Zack knew that he needed to make a sale, and Grandpa knew it would not be Smoky that was being carted off in that spanking new trailer that was bought specifically to bring home his new horse. It was apparent to the Colonel that the sellers were not amenable to parting with Smoky and was aware of why they might feel that way. There was considerable time spent with conversation flowing from both sides, with frequent pauses specifically intended for each party to present different options as well as new offers. The Colonel was by no means an astute bargainer, but he certainly was sold on his convictions. As an ex-military officer, he knew how to stand firm, and was in no way inclined to capitulate to Elmo's insistence that Smoky was staying home. This was the same man who brought victory to his side during The Great War and who would not surrender after being pitted against a larger German force. It was where he learned to apply pressure and stand resolute. The Colonel knew this was an entirely different battle, one of wits compared to one of life and death, and with opposition composed of peaceful adversaries as opposed to fanatical belligerents trained and indoctrinated to do battle with the intent to succeed at all costs and by whatever means.

In this battle of wits, he was drawn there by his own desire to make a purchase, with no forced means to make it happen. In his war experience it was required of him for humanities sake to bring supplies of arms, food, and ammunition to beleaguered American troops. In that confrontation, he was successful in carrying out his objective, as well as securing a victory that saved many lives. Today there would be no celebrations of victory and no reception of medals for meritorious achievement and heroic action. Out of this bargaining action, he wanted only one thing. He wanted Smoky on his trailer heading back home, to be safely in a stall in his stable.

His mind raced a mile a minute, and he was ready to make an offer that nobody would refuse. It was clear that his offer allowed for more value economically to the seller than to the buyer. Colonel Bob reasoned that Smoky, a horse of good age with impressive breeding lines, would help him be the winner that day.

The stage was set for the proposal to be presented and was done so in a few scant minutes. The offer was tendered to the seller and immediately drew objections from Grandpa. He had no desire to part with Smoky, regardless of what was being offered. Zack had other feelings about the proposed offer. He had concerns and obligations which did not leave room for sentimentality. He knew that Elmo had played a significant role in the acquisition of Smoky, which included the purchase of Sally at the same time. He certainly could understand why Elmo was taking such a position, but his apprehension about the future would have to be considered. He wanted to ensure an opportunity for Robbie to have a sound and profitable future in the business that would eventually become his.

It was Elmo's opinion that the sale of Smoky would adversely affect Sally since they were constant companions while out to pasture. They constantly sought each other out and visited, although separated by fence that lined both corrals. He also felt that the opportunity to breed Sally with Smoky could present some fine foals and project a prominent image of Happy Acres Farm. He shared these feelings with Zack. Although not in total agreement with him, Elmo conceded the sale was necessary and needed to be finalized.

When the smoke cleared, Colonel Bob loaded Smoky onto his newly purchased trailer. Zack discussed the attributes of the treasured items garnered from the sale. The 1928 Fordson four cylinder, three speed tractor would allow for the increase of arable land, thereby increasing the revenue from sweet potatoes and soybeans. The 1926 Model A Ford would be an answer for a second auto. The Model T, Tin Lizzie, would continue to be used around the farm and for trips into town. The speedy Model A would be used for more distant trips not possible with the present auto, and by the new drivers in the family. Elmo could not disagree with the benefits to be derived from the trade, but he was not overly excited nor happy about the loss of his Smoky.

The Colonel felt good about the proceedings, especially since he provided the family with items they needed but could not afford. He was also happy about the fact he unloaded a second car that he had no use for, as well as a rarely used tractor. Both items, used when purchased, were sold to him by a slick salesman working for the Ford dealer in the county. He remembered the feelings of "buyer's remorse" that came upon him after the purchases. *How could anyone be persuaded to engage in a purchase of two costly items in the same transaction?* He did not have the answer to that question but was thankful for the acquisition of Smoky and the long-lasting friendship that evolved with the Barrows.

Chapter 5:
Unwelcome Company

As Elmo headed over to the stable to check on things, he sensed that all was not in order. The sound of loud snorts from the horses coupled with the sound of hooves banging up against the walls of the stalls caused him to put it in high gear and get there at once. Upon entering, he was startled by the appearance of an outsider, who he did not recognize at first, nervously pacing from stall to stall. It became apparent to him that the uninvited visitor was Rolf, who had been here before.

He questioned the intruder as to what he was doing there, and what he was hiding behind his back. The answer came without delay of any sort. "Nothing, I just wanted to come to see Sparky." Elmo insisted on learning his real motivation for the visit. A nervous and frightened Rolf admitted that he was paid to put a substance into Sally's drinking water meant to cause stomach pain and possibly render her unable to perform normally for at least a weeks' time.

Elmo's questions needed answers, which were not forthcoming. Rolf did not know who it was that paid him, only that the person had picked him up along the road, and that she drove an expensive-looking black automobile. He admitted that he had ridden in the car on several occasions, each time driving by Happy Acres Farm, but swore that he did not know the lady's identity.

Rolf was advised that if the substance had the potential to physically harm or kill Sally, he would be turned over to the authorities. Rolf insisted that he had misgivings about what he bargained to do and had contemplated his actions for a considerable period of time. Elmo questioned why, if that was the case, the horses did not start acting up earlier. Rolf's explained that he was quiet upon entering the stable and did not go near the stalls to interact with them until just before Elmo had come on the scene. He confessed that he loved horses, was fond of Sparky, and could not find it in his heart to harm them in any manner. He could not cause Sally any pain or discomfort, and was getting ready to leave just before Elmo came in.

Before dismissing Rolf, Elmo inquired if he had any other information that he should know about, to which the answer was no. Rolf was informed that there could be consequences resulting from his visit once the analysis of the substance was completed and that Rolf would be contacted either by him or the police. Rolf insisted that he meant no harm and was drawn into the act by the allure of the twenty-five dollars he was offered. On parting, he was asked to report any activity or contact with anybody connected to the situation, and he assured Elmo that he would help in any way that he could. Elmo was convinced of his honesty and felt that Rolf was a victim of coercion and empty promises.

The whole of the county scampered around, completing assignments to assure the success of the upcoming festival, which was now a scant ten days away. Word around town was that Mr. Otto Schwartz, a horse breeder from the town of Celle, Germany was moving here, and would be setting up stud services at the farm recently bought from retiring hay farmer, Jack Smolder. The information received thus far indicated that he was widely known throughout Germany as a sought-after breeder and had already entered a horse in the upcoming race. Rumor had it that his entry had been declared a winner in all seven of the races in which he had taken part. The reason he left Germany was attributed to the unhealthy and threatening political climate that was brewing. Otto was said to have ambitions to start raising thoroughbreds for the purpose of getting into the racing scene. It was also known that he brought along his own jockey, one of famed repute, who was now prepping his entry, Guter Junge, at the track in Jackson, Mississippi.

The hustle and bustle extended to all the members of the Barrow family. Rose and a group of recent graduate friends were found joyfully practicing their rendition of God Bless America, with which they would open up the ceremonies. Elmo and Zack were putting finishing touches on the stage's decorations, where the preliminary activities would take place. Robbie was fully engaged in preparing for his and Sally's participation in the much-awaited horse race. Tessie and Camelia were busy working in the kitchen to make sure they had everything needed for their entries into the various food judging contests. Tessie would be baking the strawberry cake that brought her acclaim at previous Fair judging's, while Camelia would be presenting her first entry of molasses cookies that so thrilled her father. There was an air of excitement and anticipation for what everyone felt was to be the greatest Webster County Fair ever.

Rose, along with the other vocalists were at the local high school practicing for their performance at the Fair's band stage. They were made aware that they would sing prior to the Independence Day speech to be delivered by Colonel Robert Burns. All of the singers were proud to be on the same stage as a decorated war hero and were delighted that a person of his caliber and fame was chosen for the honor. The girls finished their practice session and were quite pleased with the results. Rose was preparing them for a meeting at the Fairgrounds, when her mother excitedly arrived on the scene. She could hardly find the words to inform her daughter that a letter had arrived from one of the colleges she had applied to. She just knew what was inside the envelope was an acceptance letter from the school.

Rose, equally excited at this point, hurriedly opened the letter to confirm exactly what her mother had surmised. Attached to the letter was a notification of a partial scholarship to the Agricultural and Mechanical College of the State of Mississippi, located in Starkville, Mississippi. She was overcome by emotion upon hearing of the wonderful and favorable offer granted to her. Her mother along with her singing partners offered congratulations, and best wishes for her future. Rose, aware of the time, as well as the importance of their prompt attendance, reluctantly halted the joyous revelry and informed everyone that they had to depart now.

The group left the High School, promptly boarded two cars to accommodate all of the passengers and headed to the meeting at the Fairgrounds. Upon arriving, the girls were surprised to see Colonel Burns and County Commissioner Larry Petersen in attendance. They were pleased they had been invited to be a part of a group that included a celebrated hero along with a favored elected official. It was not a case of happenstance that found them at the meeting, and being aware of this, they were all filled with a sense of pride. Tessie and the other mother who volunteered to ferry the group to the proceedings faded into the background and wandered about the grounds to get a sneak preview of some of the exhibits. Zack, who had been engaged in other Fair related business, arrived on the scene, and at once greeted the attendees and took the opportunity to introduce everybody. As the formalities were about to end, another person came ambling up to join the assembled group. He was quickly introduced as Mr. Spengler to the Commissioner, who did not recognize him.

A relaxed meeting began with Zack confirming that everyone knew their part at the Fourth of July celebration. The response from the participants affirmed that they did. Some housekeeping issues were addressed, and it was verified that all necessary equipment was available for the event. Zack informed the Colonel that a portable podium was being spruced-up and would be available to him although it had not yet been completed. He asserted that the only thing he needed was the nerve to deliver the speech.

Since there were no other house-keeping issues that needed to be addressed, Zack reviewed the timing of the program. He gave everyone a typed copy listing the sequence of events and the time allotted for each of the participants. They were instructed to be on stage before 10:45 a.m., to be careful, and to use the handrail proceeding up the rickety stairs. He assured them that Elmo had performed considerable maintenance on them, making them unlikely to be a problem. The Commissioner was informed that as the M.C., he would be the first to take the stage. He was encouraged to do as he had always done, to welcome the Fair attendees in his inimitable manner. He was to be brief and to carry out the task within a seven-minute time span, and then introduce the Guest Speaker. Colonel Bob would be allotted twenty-five minutes to deliver the all-important message for the day. He was further advised that he was not obligated to use all of the allotted time. Zack felt that having the girls perform God Bless America would be most appropriate if done so after the Colonel spoke. He was seconded on the matter by all.

He addressed Mr. Spengler and assured him that five minutes should be sufficient to tell the Fairgoers of the impending changes for next year's Fair. Rose, upon hearing what Mr. Spengler's part was, seemed satisfied with his reason for being there. Zack indicated that he had not been listed on the program due to the late request by the Fair Committee.

Zack knew exactly why Mr. Spengler wasn't listed on the program and that it didn't have anything to do with next year's Fair proceedings. Rather, it had to do with the fact that Rose had been selected to receive the scholarship award she had so wanted to win. Mr. Spengler told Zack that his daughter had scored a perfect grade on the final exam and was the only one in the class to do so. The opportunity for him to announce and present the award offered him the greatest satisfaction he could hope to enjoy. He said that additional good news came along with the award. An anonymous donor had raised the award from one to two thousand dollars, which would cover the remainder of her tuition. He was filled with eager anticipation for the time to come when he would make the announcement.

The meeting wound down when Tessie and the other driver arrived on the scene and noticed everyone preparing to depart. She alerted Zack that she had important information he would surely want to hear right away. He was taken aback by her remark and concluded that something bad had happened. His mind raced between Robbie, Grandpa, or some of the horses being victims of foul play. Tessie told him that he was about to hear news that would make him the proudest papa in all of Webster County. She shared Rose's acceptance to the Agricultural and Mechanical College of the State of Mississippi and of her scholarship award.

The news had a double effect on him, one of relief that there had been no further incidents, and one of celebration and pride for the accomplishments of his loving daughter. It crossed his mind that he could quit worrying about whether he would have the necessary resources to be able to cover schooling expenses. He was grateful for these awards and happy about the proximity of the school to home. The college was located a scant thirty miles away and would require under an hour's travel time between home and school at moderate speed. It would make for an easy, quick trip in the event one was required. He was a happy, proud, and thankful man this day.

Before Colonel Bob left the meeting, he looked to see if Rose was free to talk for a brief minute. He noticed her hugging what appeared to be the last of the girls who would be singing with her at the festivities and proceeded to walk over to her. She recognized his intentions and diverted her attention towards him to signify she was receptive to his visit. The Colonel congratulated her on the reception of the award and her acceptance to attend class in the fall. He admired her achievements and wished her much success for her future. She thanked him for his kind words and told him that she was so happy. She added that she had been looking forward to the day that they would meet and converse. She admitted to seeing him on many occasions, driving around town, at Mr. Shriner's Feed & Seed Store, and at Julie's Café, as well as at Happy Acres Farm. She guessed that they were both at these places for the same things, to buy seeds, eat lunch, and to talk with fellow neighbors. Rose took great pleasure in this conversation.

Elmo, who had been asked to stay home and readily agreed to do so, kept a watchful eye out for any suspicious activity. "Watson" felt honored by the request and was dedicated to the task. He really did not want to be bored by the proceedings at the Fairgrounds and was much more comfortable being at home. Zack found comfort in knowing that someone was at home keeping an eye on things. He was greatly concerned about the safety of his family, their home, the stable, and the horses due to the mysterious activity that had transpired lately.

When the family returned home, Grandpa, aka "Watson," relayed information about a black mystery car that had driven up to the back of the house near the stable. Just as he was exiting the stable to take Rollo for a much-needed walk, the driver had quickly reversed the car and made a quick turnaround, promptly exiting the property. He concluded that this person must have assumed the absence of both cars signaled that nobody was at home. As Robbie returned home from town where he was purchasing some saddle soap, he saw the car coming from the opposite direction but could not identify the driver due to some evasive movements that the driver made.

As they sat at the table, they all offered differing feelings and concerns they felt about the situation after hearing of these recent events. Zack's head spun much like the tops that some lucky children found left under their Christmas tree by Santa. He wondered who this might be, their reasons for doing so, and if it would bring a tragic ending. Robbie, much like Sherlock Holmes, focused on who might be the mastermind and who was aiding and abetting this person in this plan. He wondered what part each of his suspects played in the scheme. It could be the lady driving the black mystery car or the jockey hired by Mr. Schwartz. It could also be Mr. Schwartz, the owner of the new stud farm, who would soon be a competitor of Happy Acres Farm, or maybe someone that had not yet come on the scene. He also shared that he could shed some light about the strange emblem on the mystery car. His visit to the local Ford dealer garnered useful information. It was a new foreign car, the first of which was built in 1927 and the result of a merger between car manufacturers, Daimler, and Benz. The new car brand, Mercedes-Benz, featured a trademark comprising a three-pointed star encircled by a laurel wreath, which was prominently displayed on the hood. The Ford salesperson surmised it was probably shipped over by Mr. Schwartz. Tessie was concerned about what frightful event might come next. Grandpa was bewildered, and the two girls were alarmed about the whole chain of events.

It was only two days until the celebration of the Fourth of July, and the Barrow's family plans were changed from their customary routine on Sunday, which was the opening day of the Fair. They would attend an earlier church service and would not eat breakfast either at home or at Julie's café as was their usual routine. Instead, after the church service they would continue directly to the fairgrounds to partake in some of the wonderful offerings that were featured at the venue manned by the ladies from the local Garden & Food Club. Fortunately for the Barrows, it was not just a once-a-year opportunity to enjoy the food being offered because Tessie, who served as Club President, was available to provide some of the same offerings to them throughout the year.

The countdown for many who had been given specific assignments had begun. The work that still needed to be completed put some of them in a fever pitch. Zack, the chairman of the Fair, in spite of all of the alarming incidents, felt confident he had tended to his obligations. The worsening economic news did nothing to allay his concerns for his family's future, although the recent news about Rose's schooling situation tempered them somewhat. He wanted this to be the best Fair that Webster County had ever experienced and was quite sure that all of these distractions did not detract from his efforts to exact those results.

Colonel Robert Burns was pondering just exactly what he would speak about on this Fourth of July in the year 1929. It was the one hundred and fifty third anniversary of Independence Day, a celebration of a day in July of 1776 that Congress adopted the Declaration of Independence. He reasoned that he was not a speech maker and had never really delivered one. The talks that were given as a Commanding Officer were much different than delivering a speech. They served the purpose of training, educating, and informing men under his command. The material that was expounded upon was a collection of acquired knowledge about military maneuvers, training exercises, military conduct, special orders, and other necessary communication. The Colonel's speech would be a collection of his thoughts and feelings and an expression of his ideas of what the Holiday meant to him. The Fair audience would gather there because they had freely chosen to do so, unlike his audiences in military life who were directed to as a result of their service in the military. For the soldiers, it was not a matter of choice, it was compulsory.

Chapter 6:
Remorseful Reminiscing

It was Saturday night and dinner had just ended. Rose and Camelia tended to the necessary clean-up duties and Robbie was out at the stable checking on the horses, especially Sally. Zack and Tessie sat in the parlor waiting for everyone to join in and listen to the pleasing crooning of Rudy Vallée. The radio was their primary means of entertainment and proved to be so, especially when listening to the broadcast of the Grand Ole Opry, by Radio Station WSM out of Nashville, Tennessee. The end of his program was closely followed by the ever-loved Grandpa's Game to the enjoyment of all the participants. The game would not be completed this evening. Everyone was in favor of an early bedtime in order to be rested and fresh for whatever they chose to experience at tomorrow's Fair.

It was early in the day that Colonel Burns turned his attention to advice he received from one of the professors at Boston College on how to prepare a polished speech. The preparation called for the speechmaker to write out his speech, do some critical editing, and read the speech three times in order to be familiar with the content. The next step was to practice the delivery several times, with the last time performing the delivery in front of a mirror. The purpose of the mirror performance was to portray what the audience would be seeing when it was performed in front of them. It was a chance for one to detect what might possibly detract from the content of the speech.

He felt it was sound advice and would utilize it as he focused on the subject matter. The thought that some of the publicity around his service portrayed him as a hero elicited chagrin. A hero he was not. He was a soldier who had carried out orders of his superiors, which was his duty. It was the performance of a job, if you will, that he had delivered an oath to perform under all circumstances. These thoughts brought flashbacks of the fateful day that branded him a hero.

His enlistment into the Army, and his choice of the Cavalry was what had placed him in a position that required the actions he impulsively chose to take. The role of a Cavalry officer changed considerably with the advent of the machine gun and its entry into the Army's arsenal. To pursue with the maneuvers that he had spent learning and exercising for most of his military career was no longer advisable, and if performed would be a suicidal action. A rider astride a charging horse presented pure fodder for an enemy's machine gunners. There was no hiding from the withering fire that would greet them under any choice of attack mode. An attacking infantryman was forced to advance in a crouched position, gain ground in short gulps, and seek defensive cover using anything that offered protection.

Common sense necessitated the role of the horse to also change and reverted them to beasts of burden. It was this role Colonel Burns' horses were placed in as he was ordered to bring much needed supplies to beleaguered American infantrymen. What came as a surprise to him that day was that he was not only ordered to deliver supplies but was further ordered to remain and to act as an infantryman. The reinforcements that had been ordered to strengthen the weakened troops under the command of Captain Peacock were detained in a battle against a German scouting party. The perilous situation the entrapped men faced demanded that Colonel Burns' Cavalry troops remain to offer additional support.

On his arrival, Captain Jeff Peacock relinquished his designation as commanding officer and deferred to Burns, who was a superior officer. However, Colonel Burns, an officer and gentleman, told Peacock that it was not to be that way. He proposed a joint command utilizing the expertise of both men. This was the first of many moves he initiated that day that he theorized would result in ultimate victory for what appeared to be a defeated American force.

The route that brought the reinforcements and supplies to the battlefield left the detail undetected by the superior German forces. Burns told Peacock that his guardian angel must have packed the supplies. This comment was in regard to the number of machine guns that were included in the supplied material. In addition to the machine guns were several mortars, ample munitions for each of them, artillery shells, and a large quantity of small arms ammunition. The vast number of hand grenades within the shipment were treasured items, for which Colonel Burns had already devised a use. This weaponry would provide them with superior fire power.

The next day, while the two commanding officers were formulating plans for defense of their position, the majority of the troops delivered suppressing fire, halting any attempt of attacks or covert activity by the Germans. The Colonel was of the opinion that two heads were better than one and would listen and glean all of the precious information that Captain Peacock was able to provide. He requested an assessment of the current situation and was informed about the reduced troop strength of Company A led by Lt. Clyde Sparks, and Company B under the command of Lt. Peter Wysocki. In regard to weaponry, more bad news apprised the Colonel. The tank support that they had was depleted, leaving only two of them in a state of repair. The artillery officer, Captain Matt Brooks, was able to provide some semblance of good news and reported the loss of only four of their original sixteen light artillery pieces and two of their eighteen pounder mortars. The bad news was that all the artillery shells had been spent in order to repel advancing attackers. The artillery pieces had been constantly engaged for the last several days and had fired their last remaining rounds.

Peacock explained that some of the personnel and tank losses were the result of furious attacks by the German infantry, which was supported by a greater number of tanks. German artillery fire accounted for the greatest loss of men because of the lack of cover the area's topography offered.

After listening to the information that the weary officers provided, Colonel Burns informed the men that preparations for the strategy to be employed would have to be started at once. He would use the element of surprise and deception to gain the advantage in this battle, one he felt had been made possible by the arrival of more manpower, munitions, and arms. He reasoned that the German commander was likely under the impression that his army had depleted their enemy's troop strength, as well as their ammunition supply, and that the American artillery was silenced. He assumed Oberst Freidman, the German commander, believed their constant bombardment had rendered the American artillery useless. Colonel Burns felt that Freidman was now in a state of over-confidence, which would lead him to make some bad judgements.

Freidman's current plans were to rest his men for another day and then spring an attack on the remaining American troops. His assessment of the situation was that he would be attacking a heavily weakened force that was commanded by a junior officer. The Americans would be insane not to accept his offer of surrender.

The Americans' plans were set into motion, and under the advice of Burns, two new heavily concealed machine gun nests were placed in a lane that the attacking force was highly likely to approach from. His orders were to place two of the most used 30-06 caliber Lewis machine guns into the new nests. The cavalrymen would build the nests eighty yards apart, each manned by seasoned infantry members. A concealed cache of heavy explosives along with metal scraps from destroyed tanks would be placed in a pit behind each of them. When detonated, these would destroy the guns placed there and shower the attacking troops with deadly shrapnel. This would provide cover and time for the retreating American force to reach safety.

Approximately a football field's length behind the two newly built nests were six machine gun emplacements that would provide a steady stream of crossfire. This was to further deter the advancing attackers. Another set of gun placements was two hundred yards further back.

Men from the cavalry contingent were sent out to set up mortar positions in the woods that edged the open lane. They were adjusted to fire at different locations in the lane, making all avenues of approach perilous to the advancing attackers. In addition to the ones firing into the lane, two mortars were positioned to fire in the opposing direction to suppress and prevent flanking attacks.

The remaining artillery pieces were concealed from view and staggered well behind the front lines. These were not to be fired until orders were given by Colonel Burns. The decision would be made when the German attack stalled, causing a back-up of men and the tanks they were using for cover. As the stall continued, the shelling from the mortars would force the attackers to bunch up and result in more casualties when the artillery opened fire. The fresh supply of grenades would be used to forestall any chances of advancement.

The increased activity, along with the excessive noise, deluded the German command into thinking that the Americans were preparing to attack. The ruse had worked, and Oberst Freidman was dumbfounded by the radical decision that was made by a low-ranking Captain. Freidman gave the seemingly foolish Peacock the opportunity to surrender and to live, but he chose to fight alongside his men. The German Commander was angered by the decision and was determined to exact revenge on the fools who disrupted his rest prior to their next battle assignment. He ordered an attack that engaged his total force. The Americans had to be taught a lesson and pay for their insolent action.

Colonel Burns' and Captain Peacock's men assembled and prepared to advance toward the German positions. They were ordered to advance slowly to just behind the newly built machine gun nests. Freidman, because of the action taken by Peacock, hastily ordered his men to counterattack. His advancement was swift, and his troops quickly covered ground near the American zone. Peacock shouted out orders to retreat, giving the Germans the impression that the Americans did not have the stomach to fight.

The signs of the retreat emboldened the attacking force, causing them to throw caution to the wind. Burns' orders were for the gunners in the new nest to be patient. The moment soon arrived, and they opened fire as directed. An unexpected fusillade was unleashed, causing the advance to stall and the expected bunching of troops to take place. The four men in each of the two machine gun nests were ordered to return to the safety of the first defense line. Their movement was again interpreted falsely by Friedman as having no will to fight. The cessation of the machine gun fire once again emboldened the Germans to continue advancing. When Colonel Burns saw their momentum increasing, he gave the order to detonate the caches of dynamite and open fire into the advancement lane. The resultant explosions and the incoming mortars wreaked havoc on the Germans. The Americans began lobbing grenades to further disrupt and discourage the German advancement. The Germans continued to return small arms fire on the defenders but did not achieve their desired effect. So far, everything had gone according to plan, and it was now the Germans who were in a frantic, full retreat. The artillery was then ordered to open fire. Most of the retreating Germans were forced into a veritable ring of fire and those fortunate enough to escape, fled.

Six hours later, the deafening battle wound down, and the only sounds to be heard came from sporadic small arms fire. The remaining Germans were rounded up and detained in what was once their encampment. A group of reinforcements arrived and was assigned to guard duty until final determination was made regarding the prisoners' dispositions.

Colonel Burns and Captain Peacock, along with the survivors were sent to a rest area where the wounded could be given proper medical attention. The fit among them were given rest until new orders were issued for them. The artillery and tank company personnel remained with the newly arrived reinforcements to fight again another day.

Colonel Robert Burns was saddened by the revisit of events of that dreadful day and realized that he had a speech to write. His mind and thoughts would have to be centered on accomplishing that goal.

Chapter 7:
And They're Off and Running

Sunday morning, July 4th, found the Barrow family rising much earlier than usual. Grandpa was upset that he was still hindered by the annoying cast that he had to wear until the end of the week. Robbie's adrenaline was overactive and most certainly would become more so as the time for the race drew near. Rose was thrilled that Mr. Petersen had called to inform her that the singing group would sing America the Beautiful, in addition to the already scheduled God Bless America. [Author's note: History records the fact that Irving Berlin borrowed the first six notes, the one behind the words "God Bless America," from the 1906 Broadway hit "When Mose with His Nose Leads the Band"]. Tessie and her daughter, Camelia, were packing up their prepared food entries they were submitting for judging. Zack had already been to the Fairgrounds to check on everything before the family ventured on to attend church services.

A long line of early rising diners waited to get into Julie's café before heading over to the Fairgrounds. Some of the trailers that hauled horses for the big race were parked nearby, and the trucks' passengers were either in the line waiting to be seated or had already been served. An unfamiliar couple was at the end of the line, and in a very hushed manner quietly discussed race strategy. When they were notified their table was ready, the man was heard replying to the waitress in broken English. Petersen, the M.C., was seen exiting the café, and was apparently seeking out someone that he had planned to meet. He was soon joined by Colonel Burns who was asked to join him for breakfast. The Colonel emphatically replied in the negative. His stomach was in turmoil, and he admitted that he may have bitten off more than he could chew when he accepted the role of principal speaker. Petersen let out a loud belly-laugh. Surprised and amused by his answer, he swore that it was hard for him to even think that would be the case.

The Barrows arrived at the 7:00 a.m. church service and busily met and greeted fellow churchgoers. Zack felt that he was shirking some Fair duties and did not want to be attending today's services. He remembered some sage advice he received from his father when he, as a young father, did not want to attend service one day. Elmo let him know that when a leader of a band stops leading the band, players stop playing. As a leader of a family who stops attending church, you present an example to the children to do the same thing. He remembered that, because of the needs of his growing family, he found it necessary to leave his band, the Europa Five. It was a great bunch of guys, Cal on the drums, Ray on the trumpet, Ziggy on the accordion, Ralphie playing the fiddle, and Zack on the guitar. He recalled an incident that happened when he introduced Ralphie as the violin player to which Ralph responded by walking off the stage. He would not return until there was an apology from Zack as well as a reintroduction to the crowd informing them he did not play the violin. He was a country boy, and country boys played the fiddle. Zack knew what happened when he quit leading the band, they all quit playing music. That could be a sign of what may follow if he did not attend service today.

Church services were brief, which satisfied the congregation who were eager for the big day to begin. They were quickly ushered out of church and hurriedly proceeded to the Fairgrounds. Preacher Caleb just knew that they would appreciate his thoughtful consideration to dismiss early. He knew that his motivation was to get there fast and find some corndogs and roasting ears. Why, they might even treat their favorite preacher to a corndog or two for his thoughtfulness that morning.

Meanwhile, Robbie had not trailered Sally over to the grounds. She looked so relaxed and composed and he wondered whether she would get geared up to compete in the race. It might be that somebody had attempted to put something into her food or water and was successful this time. He had ample time before she had to be there for the pre-race checkup with the vet. He hoped that Sally was fine, and that Dr. Sloan had been chosen as the examiner. He would certainly detect if there was a concern.

After hooking up the trailer to the tractor, he turned toward the loading area and spotted something reflecting flashes of light. He was interested in knowing what it could be, as it was not something he had previously noticed. He hoped that it might turn out to be an object of value, but instead found it to be something that gave him cause for concern. What he picked up was an open package of Lucky Strike cigarettes. The glint that caught his eye was a reflection of the sun off the cellophane wrapper on the package. Since nobody in the family smoked, it had to be left there by a trespasser. Now his concern intensified, leaving him baffled and upset that nobody in the family had been around to identify who it may have been. An anxious and worried Robbie departed for the Fairgrounds with one question on his mind. *Would Sally, or even me, be able to compete?* He was anxious to know about Sally's condition and aimed to get her to the inspection area as soon as he could.

The black mystery car arrived at the Fairgrounds and parked in a remote part of the field reserved for parking. The car was obscured from view due to that area being much lower than any other part of the field. Two people, a man and woman, made their way to the Fairgrounds and blended in with the gathering crowd. They separated and the male continued on towards the area where the horses entered in the race had gathered for their pre-race inspection. Six of the entrants were present and accounted for. Sally and the horse entered by Mr. Otto Schwartz were conspicuously absent. It raised some questions about their absence because they were the odds-on favorites, with one of them figured to place first. Within minutes Robbie and his mount arrived on the scene.
The first sight to greet Robbie was that of Ben Snively, who was engaged in securing bets from interested bettors. Ben spent three months in the hoosegow for running a crooked betting process

when arrested four years ago by then Sherrif, Dante Sparks. There seemed to be a much more tolerant position taken by the current department regarding his previous actions. Ben lost his job as a railroad engineer and was now employed by the Sanitation Department. Questions as to whether his business was picking up became a sore spot with him. Furiously, he would respond that he was employed as a Sanitation Engineer, and not a Garbage Man.

Action intensified all throughout the Fairgrounds, and the ladies from the Food & Garden Club could not have been happier. Everyone clamored to be waited on and stood patiently in the long lines to enjoy the offerings.

The crowd was in a jovial spirit, and the air seemed to be filled with an invigorated sense of fellowship. This was the first time in the history of the Fair that it opened on a Sunday, which happened to be a holiday. The reason for the change was due to an unfortunate incident involving two of the carnival trucks that hauled the components for the Ferris Wheel. An old wooden bridge located on the route they had chosen upon leaving Florida had suffered storm damage and was under repair. This caused a two-day delay, forcing a change in the Fair dates. However, the Fairgoers did not appear to be concerned about this. The Fair would still run for three consecutive days as usual.

Mr. Bud Ransom, the carnival owner, had planned for the Panama City Fair to be his last hurrah in the business. However, he had set up for the Webster County Fair for nine consecutive years and just could not say no to doing so. He did not want to disappoint good friends, and ten sounded like a good number to quit at. He thought that since the route he took to his hometown of Nashville brought him almost directly through Europa, it made good business sense to end his career at this Fair. There was definitely a bit of sentimentality that played a part in his decision. It would have been a lot sweeter if the unfortunate bridge problem had not entered into the picture.

Bud had just signed a contract to sell his equipment to another larger carnival and felt truly fortunate about how the deal went. The looming financial climate coupled with his desire to spend more time at leisure with family and friends were the catalysts that spurred the decision to do so. It was a bittersweet decision on his part. He loved doing what he had done for twenty-eight years and would sorely miss the excitement. He had great concern for the people in his employ, most of whom were with him for an extended number of years. He would miss them dearly but found satisfaction in the fact that the sales contract he negotiated called for their continued employment. He knew that the agreement meant financial security for himself but could not help but worry about the future employment of his former employees.

Mr. Ransom, being the honest and compassionate person that he was, realized the present and impending financial climate was having an effect on the prospective Fairgoers finances. He charitably presented a proposal to offer concessions in the contract he signed with the Webster County Fair Board. The new contract allowed for increased revenue for the Fair, and also lowered the ride ticket price. He had tremendous success in his dealings and wanted to pass some of his good fortune on to some deserving and needy people. After the completion of his last venture, he would continue on to his home a satisfied and happy man.

It was nearing 9:30 a.m. and approaching the Fair's official opening and start of festivities at 11:00 a.m. The flurry of excitement was growing. The participants in the first day's judging events were astir in anticipation of the outcomes. In the pen areas, presenters were busy washing and grooming their prized animals, water fights were taking place, and some of them found solace in napping with their pets. The time was fast approaching when some lucky Blue-Ribbon winner would be burdened with the decision to sell his winning entry for a hefty price or keep his beloved pet. A group of 4H members were engaged in some self-judging, and seemed to have settled on various entries that they felt were worthy of first place.

It was that hour at which Robbie was summoned to proceed to the vet-check area to have Sally examined. The selected Vet, Dr. Bonner, after completing his examination, told Robbie that he had a fine specimen of a horse that was in tip-top shape for the race. He wished Robbie well in his attempt to take first place and felt they had a good chance of winning. Robbie went ahead to lead Sally over to the staging area where the entries were able to relax prior to the race start time of two o'clock. After getting his mount settled in, he went to the trailer to get the needed tack.

On his return to the staging area, he watched as a strong and powerful looking black stallion was offloaded from what appeared to be a brand-new horse trailer. His coat glimmered as the sun reflected off of him. Once he had been unloaded, he stood in all his majesty, with his hooves constantly pawing at the ground. His head was in a constant up and down motion, and his muscles rippled with every movement he made. Robbie was in complete awe of what he observed and in total admiration of the horse, Guter Junge. Even at his young age, he was quite adept at discerning a horse's characteristics and realized that he was going to have a battle on his hands. While looking at Guter Junge, he envisioned Sparky at five years old possessing all of the same qualities he presents. The fact that it was Sally that he would be riding offered a sudden comforting and reassuring feeling that he had the superior horse.

As he entered the barn, he was greeted by owner and jockey, Garth Sloan, who he had been acquainted with for some time. Garth wanted to know who the lady might have been that he observed walking over to Sally, and quickly departed as she became aware of his presence. He said that she could not have known that anyone was around as from where he sat, his view was blocked from her. He described her as a well-dressed and possibly affluent person. He was impressed by her riding boots and her jodhpurs that appeared to be quite expensive. She was alarmed when he approached her, and quickly turned to avoid eye contact. It seemed to him that she may have had ulterior motives. When describing her to Robbie,

Garth mentioned from what little he saw of her, he wished she were his girlfriend.

The information that Garth supplied, along with his description of the woman, did little to comfort Robbie. It was not the kind of circumstance that was welcomed, as his mind should have been focused on the race. From the corner of his eye, he caught a glimpse of a tall, well built, intimidating looking man, who he correctly identified as being the rider of Guter Junge. This man, Maximillian Brunner, acknowledged him and Garth and spoke with a thick accent of European origin. In broken English, he inquired who would be riding the mare that was entered in the race. Robbie, although proud and confident, reluctantly told him that he was the one. Brashly and clumsily, Maximillian inquired if such a young boy was not afraid of what could possibly happen in a horse race made for men. Robbie flushed and was angered by the threatening and insulting question. He was well aware of the dangers and was capable of dealing with them. Brunner grinned and turned away and said in a guttural voice, "we shall see."

Garth did not like the tone that the exchange had taken and quickly interrupted the conversation to turn attention away from the race. He asked Max where he hailed from, to which he was told Austria. Without any question being posed to him, Maximillian informed them that he had been an instructor at the Spanish Riding School in Vienna, Austria. Since being enticed by his present employer to come join him, he had been the winning jockey three times while in the saddle of Guter Junge, a winner of seven races to date. It was his learned judgement that there was no horse comparable to or capable of defeating him.

"You know," he adds, "he is just turning six in nine months. Do you realize how many broken dreams and disappointed horse owners this will amount to when racing against my mount? When you consider that he will possibly be racing for another six or seven years, that can amount to about twenty-five victories. He will leave behind seven such horses and owners today." Sarcastically he faced both of them and said, "Like we say in Austria, 'viel gluck.'" He clicked his heels, turned, and departed from what he considered inferior competitors.

Garth was glad to see him leave their company and told Robbie that he intended to ride with abandon in order to give arrogant Max a good view of his horse's rearend throughout the race.

Robbie laughed at Garth's comment, knowing he was just the one to make that happen. "I am sure his parting remark in Austrian meant 'good luck.' It's up to us to make sure that he is the one that is going to need it." He told Garth he needed to get out of that stuffy hot air and get some fresh air. They both departed wishing each other good luck and a safe ride, deep down knowing that they would have each other's back.

Grandpa, who spent his time meeting and greeting old friends, thought that he should go check on Robbie and Sally. On the way, he passed Max and a young woman. Unaware of who they were, he was impressed by their regal appearance. He wondered why they had sought out such a secluded spot between two exhibit booths to hold a conversation. He thought that maybe they were having a lover's quarrel and wanted to avoid making a scene. He figured that to be the proper way to handle such a situation as he continued on his way.

Robbie was back in the stall with Sally, softly speaking to her and gently brushing her coat. This appeared to have a soothing effect. Elmo was not surprised by what he saw because the pair had been like two peas in a pod for a long time. He walked over and told Robbie that he was going to sit with Sally and keep an eye on things while he went to attend the opening ceremonies. That suited Robbie fine as he had a craving for something sweet. His choice was cotton candy, but this would not be available until after the official opening. He meandered over to the ladies at the Food & Garden booth and saw what they had to offer. He did not want anything that would sit heavy on his stomach, so he chose a bowl of cut-up cantaloupe. After finishing his snack, which suited him sufficiently, he felt quite confident that he had made the right decision. He headed over to the area most everyone else had made their destination of choice.

The crowd gathered in front of the stage, and it was quite difficult to get close to the front. The participants were making their way on to the stage and were greeted with subdued applause and welcoming words from the audience. Robbie tried in a polite manner to edge up as close as he could to get a good view of his sister. He managed to do so and felt that he had not been impolite or offensive to anyone in the process. The hour had arrived that everyone had been patiently waiting for.

County Commissioner, Larry Petersen, shouted out a welcome to everyone on this beautiful Sunday morning, July 4th, on which America celebrates Independence Day. "It is a day that our forefathers declared our independence from a tyrannical country to become the free country that we are today. A country that we cherish, love and respect, and that many brave men have willingly given up their lives for to ensure cherished freedom for all of us." Without further ado, he introduced Colonel Robert Burns, one such hero who fought to keep America free. "Colonel, the floor is yours."

"A good morning to all, and good wishes to everyone for a healthy happy day. I, for one, along with all of you, have every reason to be happy this beautiful Sunday morning living in a free country which we are privileged to call ours. On this day we celebrate an important event in the life of this great country. On July 4, 1776, the Continental Congress adopted the Declaration of Independence. On August 2, 1776, fifty-two brave men affixed their signatures to the document, John Hancock being the first to do so. The issuance of this declaration severed political connections to Great Britain and ended ties with a country that ruled in a despotic fashion and showed no respect for the colonists.

I am both humbled and proud to stand before you today to share with you my thoughts and feelings of what my country means to me. You have just heard our gracious Master of Ceremonies, Larry Petersen, introduce me to you as a war hero. I cannot share that feeling with him for which I apologize for politely disagreeing. I am free to do so, which I will in an amicable way, because of what they accomplished that day. The action taken by the signers of The Declaration were our first steps to ensure freedom. It was to make evident that all men are created equal, possessing certain unalienable rights which include Life, Liberty, and the Pursuit of Happiness. They also paved the way for recognition of the right of petition. This further led to freedom of speech ultimately being set forth in the First Amendment to the Constitution. The form of government that we were tied to with Great Britian deprived us of these rights, making life intolerable under those conditions. This fact gives rise to our sharing a mutual love for a country, unlike most others, which allows for these endearing freedoms to exist.

To continue to share my thoughts and feelings about my country, your country, all of our country, I am going to divert to the subject of war. It is a subject that I can speak about factually due to my life experience, a subject that I have great disdain for. I abhor war, to put it simply, I do not even like to hear the word mentioned. There are three wars that I would like to address here today. The first being the Revolutionary War, although being waged as early as 1775, became the War for Independence on July 4, 1776. It was the war that brought forth the birth of this country and is viewed as a most necessary war in order to secure the freedom that we enjoy today.

The next war being the Civil War was fought in some cases with brother against brother, neighbor against neighbor, citizen of a country against another citizen of that same country. The war began with the bombardment of Fort Sumpter by the Confederates on April 12, 1861. It was a terrible conflict that ended with the surrender of Robert E. Lee to Ulysses S. Grant at Appomattox Courthouse in Virginia on April 9, 1865. The bloodiest conflict in the history of North America was fought over the moral issue of slavery. It is estimated that 620,000 lives were lost. It is a war that, hopefully, we all wished had never happened. It might not have, if in August of 1619, a government controlled by the British Monarchy, had disallowed the trade that transpired. It was a trade that took place in Hampton, Virginia, contracted to deliver food and supplies to the British privateer ship, White Lion, in exchange for thirty enslaved Africans. Several days later another ship, Treasurer, arrived with additional enslaved Africans. The traffic of seaborne slave trade was in practice in Europe fifty years prior to the voyage of Columbus to the Americas.

The Gettysburg Address, delivered by President Abraham Lincoln on November 19, 1863, set the stage for equal rights for all, requiring each man to set his moral compass in order to make it a reality. The 13th Amendment, abolishing slavery, was ratified on the 6th of December 1865.

The last struggle was the war in which I was engaged. You may wonder, 'How did it happen that I was in the military?' As a youngster, in my formative years and until I completed the educational phase of my life, I was engaged in, and thoroughly enjoyed, my connection with horses. That being the case, I figured that joining the Army and serving in the Cavalry was an answer to an enjoyable undertaking. The thought of ever having to be engaged in a war was the furthest thing from my mind. I was being selfish, interested only in pleasing myself with what I loved to do. I do admit that the time spent in the service was thoroughly agreeable with me, and enjoyable, until the decision was made ordering me to be sent into a war zone. I was not a natural born warrior and did not know if I was capable of wounding or killing an enemy combatant as the situation might demand of me.

The Great War, the war that I was engaged in, started in 1914, lasting until 1918. April 6, 1917, marked the date of the entry into the war by the United States, with the end coming on Armistice Day, November 11, 1918. Our entry into the conflict was due to the sinking of American Cargo ships, along with the ocean liner RMS Lusitania, leading to the loss of 128 American lives. President Woodrow Wilson meant to prevent future losses and convinced Congress to declare war on April 2, 1917. It became known as the war to end all wars. I am hopeful that what was said holds true, and that we are never again visited upon by the terrible specter of war. In my view, America's participation in the war was done so with total justification, and in keeping with the duties warranted of our President. With that being said, I am glad that I was able to assist in whatever small part that I may have rendered to affect an end to something so horrible.

It is my opinion that in war there are no victors, only victims.

I would like to end this speech by again impressing upon you how grateful that I am for being able to live in a free country such as ours. It did not become a free country without loyal men willing to stand up against aggression and affronts to our freedom. We as Americans, one and all, have to become that person recognized as a hero for what we contribute to that effort on a daily basis. It may be a teacher who encourages the learning of our country's history so that his or her student can share pride in what has been accomplished thus far. The one who has his or her students sing God Bless America or recite the Pledge of Allegiance to our country. It allows us to look back at incidents that left a blemish on our country. We need to utilize the knowledge learned from history that possibly may prevent us from making the same mistakes again. History is a valuable teacher, and something to remember and preserve. The hero might be your fellow neighbor performing what he does to the best of his ability to add to his neighbor's welfare. The charitable person who has a watchful eye out for a needy child or adult. It may be a father or mother who by the life they live, and the things they do, make them a model to be emulated. Our everyday life affords us the opportunity to become a hero of some sort to someone.

If I were handing out medals for heroism, I would have been compelled to pin one on each of the fifty-eight survivors who left the battlefield on a truck or in an ambulance that day in France. Any one of them would have willingly performed a heroic act if the situation warranted them to do so. Heroism is sometimes the product of someone being in a certain place at a given time, facing a situation that elicits impulsive actions to counter the threat with which they are faced.

I implore you to become a hero by doing what a free country allows you to do. If you feel like our country, yours, is going off course, cast your vote in order to right the ship. This is your country, and the person who is acting on your behalf in Congress should do what the majority of his constituents deem to be the right course of action. If they fail to act in accord with the majority, be a hero, vote them out of office. You are their boss, they are working for you, and if they are not granting you your wishes, fire them. If you are one who has not exercised the right to vote, I beg you to start doing so. One vote could possibly be the difference between achieving the desired results, or continuing to remain under an unhealthy, undesirable status quo. You young people learn all you can about the history of your great country, it will make you proud to be an American. This country is yours, do all you can to ensure the freedom that you are privileged to enjoy. Become aware of what is currently happening, try to collect all the facts, and do not allow yourself to be deluded by whatever a political opponent might say. We have no guarantee that this freedom will last forever. What we do have as citizens is the obligation to make our every effort to preserve it.

I wish everyone a healthy and happy Fourth of July, and much enjoyment at this year's Fair. Have fun and do explore the various exhibits and livestock judging available to you as a result of all of the exhibitor's hard work. You will likely bump into me if you happen to be where all of the good food is found. God Bless, and keep all of you, and thank you for your attention. Do, be a hero, protect and preserve your liberty, which if lost, may never be recovered. It was my intent for this to be a speech of short duration, for short talks are easier to remember, and I do want you to remember this one. It was my duty to present it, and it is your duty as a citizen of this great free country to act upon it."

After the Colonel finished delivering his eloquent and informative speech, he was greeted with thunderous applause from an appreciative audience, which seemed to last for over a minute. He warmly thanked them a second time for their attention and appreciation. Once again, the crowd had burst into another lengthy round of applause.

The Colonel handed it back to the gracious and eloquent master of ceremonies.

Mr. Petersen deferred to Mr. Spengler who had a brief message to deliver.

"Good day, and a Happy 4th of July to all of you. I am here today to share good news with everybody. For years, this noteworthy information was delivered in private to the deserving party. Today, I am starting a new tradition and announcing it publicly for the first time, the proper way to honor the recipient. It gives me great pleasure to introduce to you the winner of our High School Science Scholarship, Miss Rose Barrow. It was a hotly contested battle with two other competitors finishing in a tie with just one percentage point back of our winner. Miss Barrow was the only one to score a perfect 100 percent on the final exam, establishing her as the winner.

Miss Barrow, I am pleased to award this to such a worthy scholar. This is the first year that the award amount has been increased from one thousand to two thousand dollars. You are an exceptionally gifted person, and I am confident there will be other deserved awards in your future. I wish the best for you.

Please give our winner a round of applause for her commendable achievement. Thank you for your attention. God bless you all."

Rose was embarrassed. It was her hope, if she were to win, that the award would be presented to her privately. In a very shaky and faltering voice she thanked Mr. Spengler and the audience for the applause. "I will certainly ascribe to do my best in the future, not in the pursuit of awards, but rather to contribute to the betterment of our society. Thank you once more. Now I will join my friends for the singing of the songs chosen to honor this great country of ours. I hope my nerves allow me to blend in properly with the group."

Mr. Petersen returned to the stage, and promised the folks they were in for a real treat. "A group of young ladies from our fine High School are here today to present to you two of my favorite songs. Please welcome again, Rose Barrow, along with the young ladies from the High School Choral Group. They will be singing for our pleasure, America the Beautiful, followed by God Bless America. Ladies take it away."

The choral group, after their beautiful renditions, were similarly treated to much deserved applause from an appreciative and attentive audience. Perhaps Robbie offered the loudest and longest round of applause for his sister and high school friends. He was one of many in the audience who wanted more.

Larry Petersen informed everyone that it was time to end the talking and to officially declare the opening of the 1929 Webster County Fair. He hoped it would garner the reputation as being the best County Fair to date, and maybe of the future. He wished a Happy Fourth again to all and issued words of caution to be safe and to absolutely observe the ban on fireworks.

All of the exhibits were open for the enjoyment of the public. The lanes to ride the three rides on the Midway had attracted long lines. The Ferris Wheel had wide appeal among the age group over thirteen years of age, while the Swing and the Merry Go Round were just what the doctor ordered for the younger population. The fact that Mr. Ransom, the carnival owner, had arranged a deal with the Fair Committee to reduce the ticket price for the rides found wide appeal among all age groups.

The threatening clouds that started to form prior to noon time had dissipated much to the liking of all concerned. It appeared that there would be no rain on this parade today. That fact was good news for the jockeys in the upcoming race. Elmo had found things to be quiet with no suspicious activity taking place. He was now the unofficial guard for the beautiful trophy that would be presented to the first-place winner. He looked over to Sally and inquired if she liked the trophy she was about to win. Coincidently she emitted a loud nicker, almost to say that she was happy about what she would accomplish. Elmo was convinced that she communicated to him, signaling the race was in the bag. He went over to the trophy and gently stroked it. He hoped it would become the property of Happy Acres Farm. It was drawing close to race time, the premier event at the Fair. Mr. Snively was still plying bets out of some of the spectators that were there specifically to see the horse race. Although he pledged an honest betting process, he offered advice to the bettors that he felt that the foreign horse posed to be the favorite to win. That information was passed on to entice the bettor to bet that way, resulting in wagers being taken away from their original choice, which was most likely the hometown horse, Sally. Guter Junge's odds decreased, Sally's odds went up. Guter Junge would pay less to a ticket holder if he were declared the winner, while Sally would pay more. The betting would result in casting this as a two-horse race, one between Guter Junge and Sally. Snively was leaning strong on Sally being the winner. He hoped to achieve a process that had the most bets cast for the German entry, while the local horse would have lesser. He figured that all of the bets on Guter Junge would be losers, and he would pocket all of the money that was bet on him. Although paying out more money per bet to those favoring Sally, the number of bets on her would be reduced. His notion was that he would make all of this money by offering honest and fair betting to the bettor. Two hours remained until post time.

The pony rides were going over big with the crowd, and for the most part the ponies were being very placid, allowing for the rides to be constantly running with all ponies being used. All three of the carnival rides were non-stop, most likely resulting from Mr. Ransom's generosity. Colonel Burns was a happy and busy man answering questions, posing for photos, and signing his autograph on every sort of writing material he was presented with by his many seekers. "Watson" had recovered from the euphoria that overcame him when he was convinced that Sally was going to be victorious today. His whole attention was focused on one thing only, and that was her safety.

At Happy Acres Farm, Russ Inholt, a friend, and neighbor, sat comfortably in the living room of the Barrow home. He was asked to keep watch for any suspicious activity that might present itself. At this time, no sign of a threat had been noticed. There had not been any traffic, no phone calls, and his visits over to the stables indicated that all was well. Sparky, who had been let out into the enclosure adjoining the barn was frolicking in the field, galloping, bucking, and letting off steam.

The ladies at the Food & Garden Club booth were relieved that the customer flow was dwindling, and they could finally catch their breath. It appeared that when delicious and wholesome food was served, they were apt to be kept terribly busy. If one were to question any one of their customers, they would attest to the fact that it just could not be any better. Some of the interested ladies had requested that they be allowed to witness the upcoming main event of the day. With permission granted, it was off with the apron, and on to the race they went, tired but satisfied with their feeling of a job well done.

The riders had been alerted to lead their mounts out to the viewing area to allow the spectators to get a close-up view of these beautiful animals. Some of the more knowledgeable among them had concluded that Guter Junge, Sally, and another entry, Courageous Dan, seemed to be the fittest and most likely to run a winning race. The horses entered in the race offered a wide range of colors, including black, chestnut, gray, sorrel, bay, and white, and were fit and healthy looking. There were bettors who placed a bet on the horse of their choice based simply on the color, while again among the novice bettors it was based on the horses' appearance. Some made their bet based on past races in which the horse had been a winner. Then, there were a number of folks who knew the horse's owner and felt compelled to bet on his horse. Betting became frenzied, especially since the time to stop accepting bets was only ten minutes away. Although that was the case, the number of bets was considerably down from last year's betting pool. The reason was likely a result of Ben Snively's reputation. A lot of the folks were reluctant to part with hard earned money at this time, especially doing so with someone of questionable integrity.

The horses were called to proceed to the track. Some were led out by a handler on foot and three were led out by a rider on a lead pony, a horse trained for this purpose. Guter Junge was the most active among them and moved his head in a continuous up down motion, possibly to relieve a soreness or to maintain balance. They were set free from the handler and allowed to walk at an up-tempo pace and then increased their speed in short sprints up and down the track. The walking that the handlers had them doing while in the viewing area helped to get their muscles moving and their blood flowing. All betting had been suspended and it appeared that the smile on Mr. Snively's face indicated things had gone according to his plan. Sally showed no sign of nervousness in anticipation of the race, and all of the other horses behaved nicely. The Starter observed this and believed that a smooth, easy start would follow. The jockeys led their mounts to the starting point.

The horses were all lined up as directed, and the Starter waited for the point when all of the horses were completely settled so that he could fire the starting gun to signal the race was on. He felt that one horse had not yet settled down, when from the stand area two loud reports were heard. The horses reacted and the result was an unbelievably bad false start. Two young boys were led out from under the bleachers from where they set off two loud Cherry Bombs. The crowd was upset over the chain of events, and the scene became somewhat hectic. The race officials were in a tizzy over how to handle the situation. Several of the horses returned to the starting point while two of them ran the complete race. As Robbie slowly walked Sally back, he was overtaken by Max who asked him if a child in the saddle of an old mare was able to continue with the race. He cautioned Robbie that worse things could happen, which was somewhat unnerving to him. When he heard the loud reports, knowing that they were not from the Starter's gun, he immediately thought that he or Sally were targets of gunfire from whomever had been causing all of the mysterious and unwelcome activity.

All but the two horses were back at the starting point and awaiting the new start that had been decided upon by the race officials. The two finishers arrived and were shunted off to the side. After being inspected by their owners and vet, both agreed that allowing them to run the race again would not be a wise choice. The well-being of the animals was of upmost importance in arriving at the decision. The dejected owners along with two disappointed jockeys led the horses off the track, feeling very cheated by what had taken place. The two boys were led to the office selected for all Fair related business. The spectators started to settle down and once more looked for a good start and finish to the race.

The horses remaining in the race were upset, nervous, and fidgety as they prepared for another start to the race. One jockey, Jeff Thorne, had been thrown off of his unruly mount. He was not injured and wanted to continue to race. While unmounted he talked softly to his horse and gently patted him, which seemed to have a settling effect on him. Jeff remounted and sensed that his horse, Romper, was well enough to stay in the race. He knew that Romper was not favorably rated, but the thrill of the race was not going to be denied him.

The task of calming, now six, excited horses was underway. A stallion, three colts, a gelding, and a mare that a little over 4 months ago had delivered a healthy foal, would soon be thundering down the track. Excitement was building among the spectators who were anxious to get on with the race and witness the outcome. Six standardbred horses running at speeds in excess of thirty miles an hour, some with the potential for as much as forty-five, would create a lot of excitement. They would cover a distance of two-thirds of a mile in a little over a minute and ten seconds. Mr. Snively was not happy over what had transpired and knew that this had become a race that any one of the horses might win. What an unfair deal fate had dealt him.

Once the horses were settled and calm at the post, a shot rang out, and they were off. A good start catapulted six equine athletes thundering down the track with Guter Junge jumping off and taking the lead. Close behind were Sir Gallant, Jed's Hero, and

Courageous Dan, followed in the fifth spot by Sally, who was starting to make a move for a rail position. Close behind was Romper in sixth place, who seemed to be saving himself for the finish. As the horses came into the first turn, Sir Gallant pulled up abruptly favoring his left foreleg, which did not appear to be a good sign. Sally managed to get the inside position on the rail and received a slight touch of Robbie's whip to alert her to a charging Courageous Dan, who was also seeking the rail position. Sally responded to the slight flick and moved closer in towards the rail to avoid any accidental contact. Midway into the race, which now had only five contenders, it appeared that four of them were running a fast pace at this point. Jed's Hero moved up to take a slight lead followed by Guter Junge, Sally, and Courageous Dan. There was a noticeably short distance between each of the horses. They maintained this pace for another two furlongs, and with only two furlongs left in the race, Sally took a slight lead. Jed's Hero and Romper both accelerated and started to pull up to the bunched-up front runners. With a furlong left, it was Sally, Guter Junge, and Jed's Hero, followed closely by Romper and Courageous Dan bringing up the rear. The crowd had really gotten into fever pitch, and an excited bunch of enthusiasts loudly clamored for a victory for Sally. Heading into the home stretch, the jockey on Guter Junge urged his mount on, and intentionally and viciously bumped into Sally. She was forcibly slammed up against the rail, causing her to lose her stride. Garth, aboard Jed's Hero, witnessed the act and quickly responded by doing exactly the same thing to the fouling jockey's horse. Crossing the finish line, in order of finish, were Guter Junge, Romper, Sally, Jed's Hero, and in last place, Courageous Dan. Ben Snively came alive. The race had gone just as he had hoped. However, the judges quickly announced that it was a contested race, and immediately declared two horses to be disqualified for foul infractions. Guter Junge and Jed's Hero were named for their flagrant actions. The crowd cheered when Guter Junge's name was called for disqualification but did not agree with the judgment rendered against Jed's Hero. First place finisher went to Romper, second place to Sally, and Courageous Dan finished in third. The clamor and excitement continued on for a prolonged period of time. There were a lot of disappointed spectators due to Sally not finishing the race in first place. A good many of the fans were downright angry with Maximilian the jockey riding Guter Junge.

Ben Snively, in bitter despair, wondered how this could be happening to him. His ride of ups and downs, much like that of a Ferris Wheel, had come to an end, one he felt did not bode well for him. The two accountants from The Snead Accounting Firm, who were charged with computing the odds for the race, as well as securing the funds in the betting pool, were amazed at the odds disparity. They had not seen such a large difference in the odds in all the years they were in charge of calculating them. Guter Junge went off at 2 to 1, with Sally following at 4 to 1. The horse considered to be the least likely to win was listed at 80 to 1. Todd Bauer, the owner of the Ford Dealership, on a hot tip provided him by Romper's owner, had placed a one hundred dollar bet to win on Romper. A good number of gamblers in the crowd were attracted to the 80 to 1 odds, placing small bets on Romper. This fact continued to bring further unwelcome news to an already frazzled Ben.

Buddy Gibbs, Romper's owner, awaited in the winner's circle for the victorious Romper and jockey Jeff Thorne to return for the Trophy presentation. The crowd was astonished by what they had witnessed there today. Rightfully so, they showered the winner, his owner, and jockey with a well-deserved round of applause, signifying their appreciation that Guter Junge was not in the winner's spot. It was Maximillian that the ill feelings were being vented towards, not the magnificent horse. The events of the race also rendered a good many speechless and unable to express their reaction to the dangerous and blatant interference incident. They were hopeful the jockeys and horses remained unscathed. One of their home-town boys was involved, and the jockey and horse might not have fared as well as they did. The Barrow family was gathered around Robbie and Sally, thankful that each of them did not sustain injuries of a permanent nature.

As the roused crowd exited the scene, a good many of the bettors continued on towards the Fair office where the accountants were prepared to start paying off the bettors who held winning tickets. There would be a sizeable contingent arriving for the purpose of collecting proceeds from a bet they made on Romper. There would be no payouts for bets on the two disqualified horses. It had been declared that no tickets could be cashed until the vet, who had been instructed to reexamine Romper, had completed a thorough investigation. Concern over the horse's ability to finish in such a fast time raised questions. *Could it be he was administered a performance enhancing booster after his pre-race exam?*

At the meeting with the Fair officials, Dr. Vince Bonner cleared the air when he affirmed that Romper was clean of any performance enhancing drugs. As he was about to enter new facts into the equation that could possibly account for his remarkable performance, Buddy Gibbs entered the office. The doctor expressed relief that Gibbs was present and sought permission to inform the Board members of facts that he felt could lift the present aura of suspicion. He explained that as Romper's vet, two months earlier, he had treated him for a breathing problem, which was not evident at today's pre-exam. After the exam he made it a point to tell Gibbs that he was astounded by how clear his lungs sounded. He would have bet his vet's license that he would be handing Gibbs a no-go decision.

Buddy Gibbs felt that he and Todd Bauer had been prejudged as guilty of collusion due to the large bet Todd made on a horse presumed to be incapable of winning. When he visited the dealership for the purpose of buying a new car, he and Todd discussed the upcoming race. He told Todd that he was confident that his horse was the one to beat. The horse's recent performance ratings were much beyond expectations, and he only kept getting faster each workout. Buddy promised Todd that if he bet on him and lost that he would trade for a new car within a year's time. Buddy usually traded every year, so he had nothing to lose. Todd knew that fact, which he disregarded, and bet solely on the information a good friend and customer passed on to him. He felt special that he was given an inside tip.

That information made everyone in the room feel confident that everything was on the up and up. What was still a perplexing mystery was why Ben Snively was allowed to be involved with the betting considering his past history. Fran Loper, a Fair Committee member, who also served on the County Board, proposed that at the next official Board Meeting, remedial steps be taken to prevent a recurrence. She also strongly suggested a proposal that all future races be sanctioned by the Bureau of Standardbred Horse Racing, which was met with total agreement. The horse owners present at the meeting were thankful this would be put up for a vote. The word was passed on to the accountants that they could now honor all winning bet tickets.

The race crowd thinned greatly, leaving mostly winning ticket holders waiting for the payout to begin. Some of the horses, after having completed their cool down walks, returned to the trailer loading area for the return trip home. At one of the trailers, a heated conversation took place between Mr. Schwartz and his protégé, Maximilian. It was not to the liking of the latter as Otto was venting his anger over the actions taken by Max during the race. He was not happy about the intentional bumping that resulted in a disqualifying foul for Guter Junge. He was heard telling Maximillian that it was like one of the many inappropriate actions that led to his untimely discharge from the Spanish Riding School. This sort of behavior was unwarranted and would not be tolerated in the future. He told Max that he had cast a bad light on their business and would surely deter folks from wanting to do business with his new enterprise. His last remark was that Guter Junge was not a loser, but his jockey was on his way to becoming one. Max was not happy with the way the conversation ended and felt that it was a masked threat to his future.

On the first day of the Fair, attendance was greater than normal. The rides had more activity, and the food stands were all busier than usual. However, over the next two days of the fair, the crowd dwindled, and it was quite noticeable at the carnival rides despite the lowered prices. The economy had affected the current participation, but thankfully the opening day brought immense happiness to young and old alike.

Tessie was the only one of the Barrow family to bring home a Blue Ribbon that year, while Camelia earned second place in her competition. Robbie, although he did not win his race, felt proud of the combined effort of both he and Sally. He harbored no hard feelings, but certainly disapproved of the flagrant and dangerous action that affected him and his horse. His next attempt at winning would bring different results, and he thought that it could happen while riding Sparky in his first race. He liked what was proposed by Miss Fran Loper, regarding the sanctioning of the race. That would lead all participants to be more careful and mindful of the rules, thereby protecting horses and riders.

Sally Brean's hard work paid off as she won the grand prize in livestock judging. Like all entrants might feel, her attention to detail coupled with her affection for the young steer she raised, made it difficult to part with an animal she had become so attached to. She was faced with a Bud Ransom hard-to-reject offer of $500.00 for the purchase of her beloved Brutus. After considerable thought, she decided not to accept the money. It was an extremely difficult choice for her to make, especially in view of the present economic climate. Mr. Ransom was impressed by the young lady's decision and announced that he would give her $200.00 because of her devotion to her cherished animal.

The last evening of the Fair found the activity winding down with no further unwelcome occurrences. The Fair was considered to be a moderate success when measured against the previous year's numbers. The two incidents occurring before and during the race were bothersome but happily did not cause harm to anyone. In view of an impending crash of our country's financial system, the Fair was, never-the-less, a monumental success.

One sad event of the proceedings was that Mr. Snively faced trouble for not being able to honor all of the payments, one of which was the bet made by Todd Bauer. It appeared that there was some concern that a charge of fraud was being considered. It had been overheard that Todd did not intend to file charges to make that happen. Not everything ended well for everyone, but Ben hoped for a good outcome.

The conversation in the town, and County as well, was focused on the speech delivered by Colonel Burns, and seemed to have generated a sense of pride and a patriotic fervor among the youth. Bud Ransom headed back to Nashville with an inner satisfaction derived from the dealings with the Fair Committee, and with Sally Brean. He wished he would have done more, which was consistent with how he felt about the many charitable acts for which he had been recognized for throughout his business career.

It was the hope that next year's Fair would be bigger and better than ever, and perhaps would build upon the successes of this year's Fair. Mr. Ransom's participation in what was his last show, as well as his generosity to the Fair and to little Sally Brean, inspired hope for the future. The Fairgoers saw fellowship and friendship flourish among the vast audience that came to enjoy exactly that. They were a truly fortunate group able to take pleasure in all that the 1929 Webster County Fair had to offer.

Zack hoped that his own contribution to the success of the Fair would spur the next person who would be selected for that position to do even better. He sighed a breath of relief, offered a silent well-deserved thank you to all of his helpers, loaded up his car, and headed for home sweet home.

Chapter 8:
Post Race Complications

What a difference a few days made, going from the whirlwind activity of the Fair to the somewhat mundane chores called for on the farm. These seemed rather dull, and almost made time stand still. It sure seemed that way, but that feeling would pass in a big hurry. Rose was at fever pitch since there were only fifty-eight days until she was to report for Freshmen Orientation. Sally was acting as if something was bothering her and after a cursory examination by Elmo, Zack, and Robbie, they discovered swelling in her left foreleg. Elmo thought it was serious, and that the vet should be brought in as soon as possible. The feeling was mutual. Dr. Sloan was contacted, and a date was set for an examination. The doctor wanted Sally to be kept immobilized as much as possible until the date of the exam. He had two mares ready to deliver and was treating another horse for a poisoning condition, which was not responding to treatment.

A rumor was spreading around town that the bumping incident between Guter Junge and Sally may have been the result of a nasty exchange between Robbie and Maximillian. The story being told was that Robbie had insulted Max by telling him that the Austrians needed to stay in Austria. It continued with Robbie saying bad things happen to outsiders and that Max better be careful. It seemed that nobody really knew where all this talk originated from. Somebody said that she heard a young lady over at Julie's Café talking to another person regarding the matter. Questions arose about who this young lady was, why she appeared familiar to some folks in town, and why she seemed to know so much about happenings in Europa.

Elmo was dismayed at what was happening and felt surely that everything would be over once the race had been run. He thought the intimidation would come to an end. Now, he was not at all sure things were settling down and felt the family was going to have to be much more vigilant going forward. There had to be a reason for all of this activity, and they needed to find out who was calling the shots. They needed to get Mr. Inholt to be their eyes and ears again. The only thing that Elmo felt good about was that today's visit to Dr. Morgan's office shed him of that nasty cast that aggravated him so terribly. He did not intend to inform the family that Dr. Morgan was not happy with his healing process and that another appointment had been scheduled for a return visit. The doctor wanted to run a few tests. Elmo felt this was a waste of his time and informed Jane as she was setting the date for the next visit.

Garth Sloan became aware of what was being said regarding the supposed conversation involving Robbie and Max. He was having none of it and was on a mission to dispel what was being said and to bring out the truth of the matter. He was on the move letting everyone he met know the true facts of a conversation he personally witnessed. He related the incident that took place prior to the race at the Fair. Another unsubstantiated rumor had also surfaced, and implied that Rose had cheated on her final tests. Some called for her receipt of the scholarship to be rescinded and awarded to an honest person. When Rose heard of the rumor, she was devastated and could not believe that somebody would be saying something like that.

Sally was gingerly loaded on the trailer for the trip to Dr. Sloan's office for the appointed checkup. Robbie and Elmo were extremely careful so as not to inflict any further pain on a distressed, yet calm, loving pet. While the tests were being interpreted, Robbie wanted to know more about Dr. Morgan's decision regarding Grandpa's injury. It was not a subject that Grandpa cared to discuss. Robbie was insistent and finally was told information that he had never heard before. Elmo, in his youth, had the desire to become a

63

professional boxer and was touted to become a "somebody" in the boxing profession. While engaged in his fourth semi-professional fight, having won all three of his previous ones, he suffered a bad injury when landing a punch. It was intended to be a fight ending punch aimed at the jaw of his opponent, who was fortunate enough to block it with his shoulder. The combination of the violent punch landing on the opponent's shoulder as he was coming forward caused Elmo's blow to be delivered at an awkward angle. The result was a career-ending injury that continued to bother him throughout his lifetime. He was sure that the pain which continued to intensify was the result of arthritis he had had for some time. The latest injury, while mending the fence, had further aggravated the condition, and he did not need a doctor to tell him what he already knew. What bothered him more over the years was that his next scheduled bout was to be his first professional event.

A somber Dr. Sloan entered the waiting area and hastened over to the pair to inform them that he had good and bad news. The good being that the injury did not result in the need to euthanize Sally, the bad being that she had a ligament injury. She would never be able to run again. Sally would require box rest, continued immobilization, and would need to be on an inflammatory for a considerable length of time. The news was hurtful but was much easier to accept than knowing that they might lose her. Bart Sloan continued to say that the time between the injury and this exam did not do much to help the poor girl. When she was bumped in the race, Dr. Sloan noticed she changed her lead on the straightaway. The only reason for doing that was to reduce the pain in her lead leg. Continuing with the same lead would have been very painful for her. He thought that proper care would allow for some supervised walking for her, and perhaps in two months' time she would be able to walk pain free on her own. He went on to say that Sally's case and the one of the horse that he was treating for poisoning from an unknown substance had caused him much distress. He had to bring bad news to that horse's owner because he could not determine the makeup of the poisoning, and consequently, was not able to administer an antidote to counteract it. He ended the conversation in a subdued manner, extending his heartfelt sympathy. With his head bowed, Dr. Sloan sorrowfully departed.

Robbie was interested in knowing if his grandpa thought that Dr. Sloan was prescribing the right treatment for Sally. Elmo told him he thought he had always done the right thing for them in the past. After all, he was the vet and knew better than they did. Robbie pondered that statement and wondered why Grandpa didn't feel the same way about Dr. Morgan's treatment of his hand. He thought maybe this was the time to remind him that his doctor also knew what was best for him.

On the way home, Robbie realized that he would never ride Sally again. He remembered thinking, after the race, that it would be Sparky that he would be riding at next year's Fair. A sudden flush of anger overcame him when he became aware the injury had come from Sally's leg contacting a fence pole when she was bumped. *Why would someone intentionally want to inflict pain and suffering on his beloved horse?* He began to harbor ill feelings towards Maximillian and also wondered if the bumping incident could have been ordered by Otto Schwartz.

Shortly after arriving home, they received a telephone call from Colonel Burns, who was concerned about what he considered to be malicious talk aimed at the Barrow family. He wanted all of them to know that he, for one, was upset at some of the remarks he heard. The Colonel went on to say that he knew deep down that none of them were of the mind to do any of the things they had been accused of. He was firmly in their corner and would stand with them until everything was made right. He inquired about Sally's outcome at the vet and offered his regrets upon hearing the news regarding her condition.

At the new stud farm, a discussion regarding Maximillian's recent antics had Otto in somewhat of a rage. It was hard for him to believe that he would commit a foul, such as the one at the race. Max was told that he had not learned any lessons from his release as an instructor at the riding academy. Otto encouraged Max to take advantage of the opportunity that he had been presented with. As he was advised at the time of his hire, he had been given the chance of a lifetime. He was not considered an employee, but a household member. He knew that Otto had no family ties, and that he would likely be heir to everything if he rehabilitated himself and presented the appearance of a gentleman. These were Otto's wishes. Max was sternly reminded that it was up to him to make it happen. The last bit of business of concern to Otto was that in his short time in Europa, Max was back to chasing women, a practice that led to some of his earlier problems. He did not like the idea of Max's newly found female companion driving the Mercedes that was bought for him. Max had no reply, which Otto waited for, and left the meeting with a dark cloud hanging over their discussion.

A rendezvous between Max and his mystery woman was set to take place at Julie's. At the appointed time, they were found conversing about the nature of his meeting with Otto. Chantele listened intently for Max to provide her with the content of the discussion that took place. They exchanged views and thoughts about everything that was said, then paused for what seemed to be an eternity. She then began to demand certain actions on his part. She didn't like the idea of Otto's resentment regarding her driving the Mercedes. Max was to assert himself and notify Otto that he was not a child and should be able to have the woman he loves drive his car. From what Max had told her, Chantele surmised Otto had already decided to take him out of the picture as a potential heir. He needed to start thinking of what he planned to do to ensure he would end up with all of Otto's possessions.

After the meeting, the two parted and Max was left to consider all that had just transpired. His first thought was the lack of appreciation that Otto displayed regarding all of the bad publicity floating around town regarding the Barrows. Both he and his new lover were trying their best to alienate potential customers from patronizing Happy Acres Farm. They reasoned that the customers would be swayed to do business with the new stud farm being operated by a man with noted credentials. His mind was full of thoughts, and he had no idea of what he should do.

The following week, Grandpa was back for his follow-up exam. Dr. Morgan viewed Elmo's x-ray. What he initially thought was damage from his recent accident while repairing the fence, actually included injuries from Elmo's boxing accident that had never healed properly. The recent injury was aggravated by the former injury, accounting for the pain, as well as the slow healing of the sprained ligament. It would take considerable time for the sprain to heal, and it was crucial that he not use his hand for anything requiring exerted effort. The new injury would also cause the existing arthritis to become more problematic.

Back at the house, Zack entered and presented a look of dejection. Tessie immediately noticed and inquired as to what was wrong. The answer was not good news, as Zack informed her of his loss of employment. He had been told he was no longer needed. The slowing economy was forcing the owner of the farm to reduce costs, and this was his first step in doing so. Zack wanted to know if any of the rumors that were coursing throughout the town had influenced the decision, which he was told surely did not help. They were dumbfounded and could not find reasons that made them the target of all the falsehoods.

Rose was at home getting her clothes and other articles ready for her move to the dorm. She was in a state of mixed emotions, excited about the thought of being a freshman in college while also feeling down in the dumps over leaving home. The telephone rang and the message she received added a few more emotions. She was suddenly overcome by bewilderment and fear. Her classmate, a waitress at Julia's Café, informed her that her old nemesis, Chantele Dubois, was back in town. In fact, she had been to the café several times, but her classmate did not readily recognize her. It was no wonder, since she had restyled her hair and dyed it black. She had also changed her name to Betty Black, at least that was what she was being addressed as now. Her loss of weight added to the reason that she was not immediately recognizable. She was talking to one of the old chums she used to associate with when she slipped and called her by her given name. That brought a lot of hushes from Chantele, who was quite upset with her friend for doing so. When Rose inquired as to whether the falsehoods circulating throughout town were coming from her, the answer was an emphatic, "you bet."

The conversation took a turn and became centered around the jockey that bumped into Robbie's horse. Chantele and he had been seen together on numerous occasions. She had been seen driving his car without him present and had to have been the one who sideswiped Robbie while hauling Sally to the Fairgrounds.

Rose, vividly upset, wondered what steps she should be taking now that would not reflect negatively back on her. She was afraid to say anything that might be misconstrued by someone that had been influenced by the nasty lies. She was told not to do a thing. The girls in her circle of friends had already set up a plan to confront Chantele, and they did not want Rose to be involved.

Chapter 9:
Rose's Dilemma

She felt it was time to seek her father's advice as to what needed to be done in order to get things right. Zack and Rose sat at the kitchen table, where Zack half-heartedly nibbled on a sandwich that he had just prepared. He had no appetite for food and wondered why he even made the effort to do so.

Rose was worried and frightened and sought good advice from her father. She asked, "Dad, do you have time to help me sort out all that is going through my mind?"

"I always have time for you, and you should be the first to know that."

Rose continued, "Your advice to all of us children has always been sound and helpful throughout our lives. The one bit of advice from you that stands out to me is you saying, 'Whatever you do in life, you should do to the best of your ability.' I have made that to be a goal in my life and now I look back and it seems that by doing so, I have created a problem."

With a puzzled look, Zack wondered, "Just exactly, what do you mean by that? I don't understand how doing right can cause problems."

"I never bothered you with some of the issues that I encountered with Mr. Dubois' daughter, Chantele. Throughout my last year in elementary school, and into the first two years of high school, things had developed setting her and I on a collision course. I thought that when her father accepted a promotion in his job and moved the family to Jackson that the problem had gone away. I had never felt such great relief as I did when she was removed from the scene."

"What went on between you two that I should have been made aware of?"

"Chantele was jealous of my achievements. It all started in eighth grade when I won the American Legion Essay Contest. She felt that hers was better than mine, and that I had received help from our teacher. She would not let go of her feelings on the matter and constantly referred to me as a cheating liar. The next two incidents took place in high school during physical education classes. The first was when I scored the winning goal in a game of field hockey and was swarmed with appreciative team members. The second was when I finished first in a 100-yard dash, narrowly beating her to the finish line. In each case she belittled me, and in the more recent incident, I was sternly advised that it never happen again. She made every effort to make life uncomfortable for me, and in some cases, she was joined by some of her friends in doing so. I was not purposely trying to outdo or upstage anyone, I was merely competing and trying to do the best I was capable of doing."

"Rose, you did exactly what everyone would strive to do in those situations, and assuredly, it is what I would have expected of you."

Zack was of the opinion that the time had come to do what should have been done at the time of each incident. "The first thing you should know is that you did not cause her to be the person she has become. Rose, you should approach Chantele and tell her exactly what you have just spelled out to me. The first step in resolving a concern is to engage in honest dialogue with the person involved. That action usually results in promoting an understanding of what caused the differences and highlights the error of one's way. If you do not achieve success in resolving the issue with Chantele, I would approach Mr. Dubois, who I feel is a very reasonable man. You should make every effort to mend fences with her if that is at all possible."

"Dad, I can assure you that I did try to explain my side to her, but she refused to engage in conversation. All that I received in return for my comments were unflattering and degrading remarks from her. She is not an easy person to deal with and can become very volatile at times. I am going to do as you suggest. Hopefully, she may have a change of heart and some good might come from the meeting. I love you and always appreciate and find wisdom in your advice. Wish me luck."

Rose was quite confident that she might just find Chantele at Julia's Café and prepared to go into town. When she arrived, Chantele was not there, but she did find several of her faithful classmates just about to leave. Upon seeing Rose, they turned around and followed her into the café, which was not at all crowded. They all gathered around a large table and informed Rose of their encounter with Chantele. They had convinced Chantele that they, and many others, were on to what she and Max were trying to do by spreading these false rumors and shedding a bad light on the Barrow family. Chantele did not respond very well to what they had to say and left in an angry mood. Upon leaving, she advised them to stay out of her business, because meddling any further would cause unwanted consequences. She was in such a rage that she left a full pack of Lucky Strike cigarettes behind. The girls were of the opinion that she was to be considered a dangerous threat to Rose and cautioned her to be careful.

"Oh, I will be careful," Rose assured them, "But I would like to arrive at a resolution to this festering problem. I am of the mind to continue until I achieve those results."

Chapter 10:
A Call to Action

Rose left the Café, more concerned than ever, and headed to the farm of Otto Schwartz, feeling that Max might be there. She was hopeful she could convince him to help her smooth things out with his new lover. It was a chance she was compelled to take.

Max was there, and he was not alone. He was with a cunning young lady who had led him to become an unwilling accomplice in a tangled web of intrigue. Rose knocked on the door expecting to be greeted by Otto. Instead, it was an extremely nervous Max who greeted her. She was quickly invited in at the insistence of none other than the person she was looking for. It was not a welcome greeting that she received from Chantele, who quickly grabbed her and slammed the door shut behind her. Max was ordered to take Rose and lock her up in the guest bathroom. He did so with little hesitation, but in a gentle manner. Rose felt that he was not a willing partner and thought maybe there might be some hope for her well-being.

Rose heard scant bits of the conversation taking place between the two and was able to hear Chantele tell Max that he was "in this up to his neck." She advised him that she was giving the orders, and it was to his advantage to recognize that fact.

All the time she was confined, Rose wondered what was in store for her. *Was she to be left locked up with no way to escape, in what would be an abandoned house? Would anyone come looking for her, and where was Mr. Schwartz while all this was taking place?* Little did she know that Otto lay in his bedroom in deep pain from a poison that he ingested while eating a left-over piece of pork. The meat was lethally seasoned for him by Chantele with poison she had intended to administer to her father. Her father was fortunate he had been suddenly picked up by his driver, right after telling her that she was no longer welcome in his home.

There was no way out for her, the solid wood door could not be broken down, and it was locked from the outside.

Maximillian was bewildered. *How could he arrange for Rose to escape, find Otto, and seek medical aid to prevent his death?* Meanwhile, the mastermind was barking orders at him and wanted him to check on Otto to make sure he was incapable of taking any action to seek help. Otto's death would be considered accidental, a result of food poisoning.

Chantele knew she had to provide an explanation for Rose's demise. She had to present a solution to the problem that would not cast doubts or raise suspicions. If they fled the area, they would become immediate suspects. The answer was to go to town to be noticed so as to throw off suspicion that they were at Otto's when Rose came. She would have been invited to share some left-over pork with him. They would explain that she came while Max was out for a ride in the country with his girlfriend, and later to get a bite to eat at the Café. One thing was missing from the plan. She had enough poison left to complete the job, but the pork was gone. Chantele thought that if she used some other way to ingest it rather than forcing her to eat the pork, a medical check would bear out that fact. She decided it was best to buy more pork. It would only take one small chop to do the job. Rose was going to pay for making Chantele's life so miserable.

While Chantele was preoccupied with her dilemma, Max figured out a way to get a key to Rose. He inserted a key into a roll of toilet paper and slipped into the bathroom to inform her what he had done. Max warned, "Don't try coming out right away because she may still be outside checking on things. Otto is in his bedroom and has been poisoned. Get immediate help for him."

Chantele was thoroughly satisfied with her plans and sought out Max, checked on Rose in the bathroom, and made sure the key was in the lock to prevent Rose from possibly picking it. Max was able to pull the key out a bit without being detected as the couple went out to head for town.

After waiting some time, Rose inserted the key into the lock, but it would not turn to unlock the door. Several more attempts brought the same results. No matter what she tried, nothing worked. Her major concern was that she could not get to a phone to call for medical help to aid Otto. She reasoned the key on the other side of the lock must not have been pulled out far enough to allow for her key to turn the tumblers. She softly murmured, "Please, somebody come help us."

Max and Chantele were sitting at a table at the café and drew a lot of attention from several of the customers. They seemed to be in a heated exchange with most of the conversation spewing from her, and in loud voices at times. Max appeared to be extremely uncomfortable and was pleading with her to tone down her voice. Julie, who was becoming suspicious of their actions, beckoned one of the waitresses to come over to her. "Jennie, I want you to go over and wipe off some of the tables near them and be sure not to make it appear as if you are eavesdropping."

Max did not like Jennie being so close to them and told Chantele that it was time to leave. There was no argument on her part and they both walked out trying not to attract further attention.

Jennie hurried over to Julie and told her, "I heard Max say, 'What about Rose,' to her."

The phone rang and Julie answered to hear an excited Robbie asking if Rose was there. He noted, "She has been gone for almost five hours now, and we have no idea of where she may be. My dad is terribly concerned."

"We are also, as Max was just heard asking Chantele, 'What about Rose?' They just left the restaurant, and it sounded as if they intended to go to the stud farm." Julie also mentioned a detail from earlier in the day. "They left a package of Lucky Strike cigarettes. Rose had said it was information you should be aware of."

"Thank you, that information narrows down our list of suspects to three people now: Chantele, Max, and Otto. Julie, would you call the police and let them know what the situation is? Please tell them to hurry to the farm. My grandpa and I are leaving for there right now and I believe we can get there before they do, if in fact that is where they are heading."

Zack, who was in turmoil, could only sit and wonder while asking Tessie, "Why did I suggest she go to try to make amends? I believe I may have put her in danger. Something must have gone wrong because it is very unlike Rose to be gone for so long, and not be back in time for the family dinner."

Zack knew he must remain at home should she return home or try to call for help.

The town was alive with activity. Colonel Burns, after having been notified, gathered a group of townspeople to start a search of the area in and around the whole town. "I know there are rumors going around concerning the Barrow family, but it is time to rally around a family you have known and trusted for most of your lifetime. Let us, as friends and neighbors, go about this in a proper way and seek a just answer to the immediate problem confronting us. We need to find Rose before it is too late."

Robbie and Elmo arrived at the farm. There was no sign of Max or his car, and they felt relief since they must have arrived before Max and Chantele. "Grandpa, why don't you go around to the back, and I will try to enter from the front."

A knock on the door brought no response from anybody that might be inside the house. He tried knocking several more times, harder and louder each successive time, but there was still no answer. Upon trying to enter, he found that the door was locked. Just as he was deciding his next plan of action, Grandpa, who entered from the rear, opened the door for him. Robbie entered and shouted out in a loud voice, "Is anybody home?"

A joyful Rose answered, "Robbie, it's me! I'm locked in the bathroom. Call Dr. Morgan. Otto has been poisoned and needs help. Tell him to hurry. He has been crying out in pain."

Robbie quickly reacted and made the call. Jane, Dr. Morgan's nurse answered, and Robbie informed her of the necessary details, except for a question he could not answer. Jane needed to know what the poison was that Otto was given. He did not know.

"Wait a second, Jane. Elmo has a medicine bottle in his hands. This might be the answer you are looking for."

It was, and Robbie hung up the phone and made his way to free Rose, who was already in a bear hug with Grandpa. Sirens were wailing, and two fast approaching police cars arrived. Otto was found to be in much pain, although very coherent considering what he had been through. Rose, who was the first one in the room, told him, "Dr. Morgan will be here very soon, hang on."

Another automobile was seen approaching and appeared to slow down, before the driver, Chantele, accelerated and continued on past the house at a high rate of speed. She knew that her only hope now was to evade capture. Max pleaded with her to stop and surrender.

Chantele ignored his plea. "Max, you dolt. Don't you realize that if Otto has passed away, we will be facing murder charges? If he has not, which I hope to be the case, the charge will probably be attempted manslaughter. The poison that you gave him was slow acting, and he most likely will live if treated in time."

Max argued, "It was you that fed him the poison, not me."

"Who do you think the police will believe, a man who committed a foul in the horse race and caused a horse to never be able to run again, or an innocent lady involved against her will?" Chantele retorted.

"You would probably poison me after you got what you wanted," Max pointed out.

"Wow, you catch on fast. That's the first intelligent statement you have made since we met," she said sarcastically. "Why are you so insolent?"

Max had the last word, telling Chantele, "You are the one who is not too smart. Don't you realize that the person you kidnapped has just been rescued by the police? She is going to have a lot of information for the authorities, and your actions will result in a charge of kidnapping, to go along with the other counts against you. Your hatred for her will end up bringing you much to regret. I might just visit you in prison if they don't give you a death sentence." He chuckled and added, "I wish you good luck, you are going to need it."

Dr. Morgan administered the antidote needed to counteract the poison and felt assured that Otto would be up and around in a few days and good as new. He turned to Robbie to praise him for his quick thinking. "You should know that you and your grandpa are to be credited with saving Otto's life."

Grandpa joined in on the parade and credited Robbie with making all the right decisions and wondered how a young man came up with the right answers. Robbie, who felt not at all deserving of what they say he accomplished, jokingly told Grandpa, "It's elementary, my dear Watson."

Chantele and Max didn't get far. There were a lot of heroes involved in their capture, including the Colonel, who mustered the citizens much like he mustered the troops at the battle in France. At the Fair, he implored his audience to become heroes, and they responded accordingly. The citizens answered the Colonel's ardent plea and quickly managed to apprehend the suspects by blocking off any and all routes leading out of town. A beautiful ending to an ugly episode in their lives.

Maximillian Brunner, and Chantele Dubois, were in custody awaiting arraignment in court. A date had been set for ten days from today. Both Chantele and Maximillian pled not guilty to the charges filed against them. They would be tried for their alleged crimes three weeks from this date.

The Barrow family members were safe, and together they gathered for a reunion with Zack, Tessie, and Camelia to enjoy the peace and solitude that home sweet home offered them. All is well that ends well.

Chapter 11:
Venturing Out

The mystery, and the danger that was a part of it, was thankfully a memory of the past. Now it was time to focus on the future. Rose was putting together the last of what she would be taking with her to her first semester of school. It was the classical and scientific studies that were offered there that interested her, and it was her academic achievements that attracted the interest of the Admissions Director of the college. The college had found a potential phenom in the person of Rose Barrow. She was the type of person that would, in time, influence other young prospects to secure their education there. A win-win situation for both parties.

All necessary preparations had been completed. The family as well as the luggage were aboard, and an excited group was on the road to Starkville, Mississippi. It was the first all-family venture there, and it was also the first trip for the Model A Ford, the same one tendered as barter in the trade for Smoky with Colonel Burns. The conversation was somewhat subdued due to the mixed emotions of the passengers. Rose was filled with anticipation, a sense of loss, and a sense of excitement, all of which made her the most talkative. Zack and Tessie were filled with pride for their precious daughter, mixed with sorrow of having to leave her alone at school. The other three were plain sad and busy looking at the unfamiliar sights as they motored on. Robbie excitedly blurted out, "Grandpa, did you see that horse running along the fence line while keeping up with our car? We need to stop at the farm on the way back and get a good look at him."

Zack looked back at him and said, "I believe that's a good idea. Watch for a road that leads up to the place."

Rose questioned, "Am I going to be replaced by a new horse?"

Camelia laughed and added, "Well, Rose, you never were able to run that fast."

The time passed rather quickly and soon they reached their destination. The buildings were rather impressive, and the grounds were beautifully manicured. Flowers of every variety abounded. The grass was lush and freshly mowed, giving credence to the fact that this was an agricultural college. It was a very inviting and splendid sight to behold, and most assuredly cherished by students attending classes. It seemed to Rose to be a place that she would enjoy and that was reminiscent of the farm.

The first order of business was to find the Office of the Registrar, register for classes, and find out what dormitory she had been assigned for her lodging. They secured the information and drove to a most beautiful building that graced a large plot of ground featuring an emerald lawn with plush trees of several varieties. A large number of flower gardens were spaced throughout the property, adding to the beauty. It looked as if it was a castle found in medieval England. She was well pleased with what she saw and was anxious to see the inside of the building.

She found the interior of the building to be very appealing and was delighted with her dorm room. The furnishings were in good order, and the room was painted in ecru tones, with a soft blue color on the woodwork. She noticed it to be quite cheery and homey. "I do believe that I am going to like it here, but I'll find it difficult being separated from all of you. The lady in the Admissions Office said that the cafeteria is open for short hours and will close at six o'clock. They have been operating on a limited menu basis for the last three days, but she did say the food was good. She let the staff know that the Barrow family would most likely eat there today and also called for there to be no charge for our food this evening."

The early dinner, the last they would eat together for several months, was very satisfying and they were grateful for the hospitality provided by everybody.

Zack announced, "The dinner was particularly good, but falls short of measuring up to your mother's cooking. I am satisfied that you will be well fed, and the vegetables coming from the college's gardens will be fresh and healthy. I might just learn a thing or two if we stick around much longer. I would like to continue on our tour of the campus if that suits everyone."

Rose was highly in favor of the suggestion and could hardly wait to get going. "Let's get the show on the road, we're burning daylight."

A happy and excited family spent the next two hours viewing all that the campus grounds had to offer. There was never-ending praise for the beauty to which they were treated. Robbie was impressed and added, "This very well may be where I end up someday. Perhaps they will offer courses on animal husbandry by the time I am searching for a college to attend."

The sun would be setting shortly, and it was nearing the time for goodbyes. The last stop was back at Rose's dorm, the place that she would call home, for at least the next four years. Tessie was having a hard time saying goodbye, and Zack was shedding tears. It was difficult for all of them to part company, but there was no alternative. Rose put on a happy face and tried to cheer everybody up, so the parting would be easier to accept. Zack informed Robbie that they would not be able to stop at the farm where they saw what they felt was an extraordinary piece of horseflesh. "It would not serve any purpose other than to get a close-up view of the animal. I know you were thinking that perhaps we might be able to make a deal to secure that beauty, but the fact is, we do not have the means to do so presently."

Grandpa added, "We have a bunch of animals back at the farm, some of which might be needing attention now. I do believe that we should get on the road."

A brave and lonely looking Rose waved goodbye as the car slowly departed for the return journey home.

Zack drove away, proud of Rose and confident she would do well in her new home. "You know Tess, we have done a good job raising three fine children, and they all know how to care for themselves. I don't think we have anything to worry about for the well-being of any of our children. Rose will be fine."

"I know that's the case, Zack, but it will take time to get used to her being gone. I miss her so much already. When I reflect back on what the last several months have brought us, I am just so thankful that she did not come to any harm."

Zack replied, "I'm happy that Robbie did not end up injured, and proud of what he and Grandpa did to end things in a safe manner. We have a lot to be thankful for."

The weary travelers returned to find that all was well. Several of the horses needed to have their water replenished and faithful old Rollo needed some attention. Grandpa called to him, and he came bounding over, almost knocking him off his feet. "Whoa boy, you need to settle down, and quit waving that tail of yours. Do you want to cause a dust storm?" They all take care of whatever requires attention, and a tired bunch get ready for a good night's sleep. Before retiring, Robbie asked Zack if maybe they could do some bartering to secure the horse.

"We can address that tomorrow when we can all think clearly about the issue." It was sleep that interested Zack presently.

Chapter 12:
An Unheeded Warning

It appeared that fall would be much cooler this year. The leaves were already falling from the trees. A beautiful bright sunshiny day was in store for the family as they got ready to sit down for the first breakfast without Rose.

It did not seem right without Rose there, and Camelia was the first to say, "It feels so lonely without all of us being together."

Tessie explained, "We are going to have to accept that fact and keep her in our thoughts and prayers."

Before anyone else continued the conversation in that same vein, Zack interrupted, and said, "We certainly are a fortunate family, a bad time in our life has ended. Rose is in college, and we are all healthy and doing well. It's time for us to count our blessings and get this day off to a good start."

Rose, an early riser, was the first to arrive at the cafeteria for her first breakfast away from her family. She placed her belongings at a table off to the side of the room and waited a few minutes for other students to arrive. After several had entered the line and were being served, she decided it was time for her to do the same. The choices she had made were very much like the food she was used to eating at home. With her tray sufficiently filled, she returned to her table and sat down alone. It was not long before she was joined by a pair of young men who wanted to be the first ones to meet the first young lady to attend the school.

"Hi, I'm Joel, and this is my friend Denny. You will find him to be unusually shy and quiet at first, but once he gets comfortable with somebody, they wonder whatever happened to the shy guy that they first met."

Denny fired back, "Oh Joel, you introduce me like that all the time." The conversation flowed rather easily between all three of them, and then the bell sounded for their first class of the day. They departed with the usual pleasantries, and each headed off in a different direction.

Zack had not broached the subject weighing heavy on Robbie's mind, that of the fine specimen they saw traveling to Starkville. Robbie was having difficulty concentrating on his chores and wanted to know what his dad's thoughts were on the matter. He figured that if the subject did not come up before lunch time, he would address it while they were eating lunch.

Zack and Elmo were seated on the bench in the stable area, where they felt that their discussion would not be overheard.

"I am trying to keep my concerns away from the rest of the family, but you must have noticed the drop off in our crop sales. We also have not been doing much good with our stud business or in sales of yearlings. Sallie's vet fees set me back a good bit, and costs for her current care do not help the situation. I am very worried about our future; the economy seems to be heading for a tumble. With the loss of my extra job, it has put a strain on the cashflow."

"I know that, Zack. I have seen it in your face, and it has bothered me considerably. I have been giving some thought to clearing some more land to increase our soybean production. It is the one crop that we can be assured we will be able to sell all of what we raise."

"It makes sense, Dad, but can you take on that job?"

"I'm not doing the work; the tractor does the work. All I must do is steer the blamed thing."

It was time for lunch, and two hungry people were on their way to the first meal cooked by the new chef, Camelia. Rose's replacement had a lot to live up to, having to satisfy a group who had feasted on Tessie's and Rose's superb cooking. Robbie came in a little later. He was late in completing his normal chores as he could not get that horse out of his mind.

The table was nicely set, and the aroma that filled the kitchen was enough to satisfy any questions or doubts that her family may have entertained. The short ribs that she served were not their usual fare and they were totally delighted with the meal.

"Camelia, make sure to choose this dish as your entry in next year's Fair."

"Now, Dad, you know this is not as good as what mother would have prepared."

"Don't sell yourself short, young lady."

The conversation was all about food, and Robbie wanted to talk about an entirely different subject. He wondered when that conversation would be brought up. He could not wait any longer. "Dad what have you decided regarding the horse we saw?"

"Nothing yet, I have to sort some things out before I am able to discuss the matter any further."

Robbie questioned, "What sort of things?"

Elmo pleaded with him to be patient, and they left to finish the rest of the day's work. He jokingly said, "I have to get all the work I can out of you today. Tomorrow starts your first day of school for the year."

The next day Elmo planned to attend to some business that he had been neglecting. He intended to visit the owner of the horse that Robbie wanted to acquire. Upon informing the owner of his desire to purchase the horse, he was told it could be possible. Mr. Branson wanted to know the reason for his interest in the horse, and Grandpa told him that was for his grandson. After much small talk, Branson explained his reason for possibly selling, and what he would like in return.

"Rusty is a spirited horse, too much horse for my daughter who has a leg problem. What I am looking for is a horse that would suit her needs. The horse has to be calm, not prone to galloping off wildly, and one that she can learn to love. If I could find that horse, I may be willing to trade even."

Elmo offered, "We have just what you are looking for, a four-year-old, with a leg problem which is on the mend. She had a ligament injury that has healed nicely and has been declared unable to run again. In another couple of months, she will be able to accept a rider. She has a great temperament and would suit your needs perfectly. I'll give you assurance that she is fit to perform before we engage in a sale. I would like you to have your vet perform a fitness exam to ensure there are no medical issues. The hitch in the deal from my side is if my grandson will be willing to part with Sally."

They both agreed that each of them would get together once there were no complications hindering their exchange. Elmo thought this news may be of interest for Zack and Robbie.

Another school year arrived for the students at the local high school and Robbie and Camelia were on their way to begin their sophomore and junior years. It was a nice warm day that saw them heading off to another year of schooling. Robbie was remorseful because he was not riding his faithful friend, Sally, to school. Camelia was concerned over the fact that her dad and Grandpa were left alone to do all the work.

The date for the scheduled arraignment drew near and over at the jailhouse one of the guards approached the head jailer about a concern he had. He reported that he saw Chantele and another guard fraternizing. The head jailer wanted more information.

"Who is the guard that you say is involved, and what have you seen?"

The informer responded, "It is Rogers, the new guard. I saw them in an embrace and kissing."

"I find that hard to believe. I know the Rogers family and they are a decent family; I just do not see that happening. Are you sure it was Rogers you saw, and not someone else?"

"I am almost positive it was him."

The head jailer exclaimed, "I don't believe it was Rogers that you saw, and you yourself don't sound too sure that it was him. I want you to keep an eye out for any suspicious activity that you might see. Oh, in the future please be positive about who it is you report."

Ben Snively's day in court arrived. He was not charged with any wrongdoing, although he had been sternly advised he would no longer be able to participate in the betting process at the Fair. He paid Todd Bauer, the big-ticket holder, one half of the winning amount, and Todd excused him from the responsibility of paying the total amount. It seemed everyone in town was happy about the outcome for Ben, and Todd had become somewhat of a hero due to his benevolent gesture.

Meanwhile, Elmo had Sally checked out by Dr. Sloan, and he was quite happy with the vet's assessment of the progress that she had made since the last visit. Dr. Sloan thought that she was healing much faster than he had anticipated. He advised that the therapy and the treatments continue as planned, and in another month, she would be ready for a saddle.

The additional land designated for the purpose of increasing the soybean yield was progressing nicely. Almost seventy-five percent had been cleared, but a snag developed preventing further progress. Clearing of the remaining portion of land had become more problematic. The roots of previously cleared large shrubs were rather difficult for the Fordson tractor to remove. Elmo decided he was content with what he had accomplished and reasoned that the remaining portion be cleared next season. If all of the beans grown were sold, it would make sense to go about clearing more land.

Chapter 13:
The Great Escape

A harried guard once again informed his superior that he had information for him. Chantele, with the help of young Rogers had escaped. They were both missing, and one of the other guards said he saw what might have been both of them getting into an automobile. The jail was put on lockdown in order to prevent anyone else from escaping. The Sheriff issued an order for an all-points bulletin to be on the lookout for the pair.

When Julia opened the door for business, she found a note stuck between the door and frame. The note was addressed to Rose containing this message.

THEY WON'T BE ABLE TO FIND ME, BUT I WILL FIND YOU. YOU WILL NEVER KNOW WHERE OR WHEN. SLEEP WELL.

Julia called Zack Barrows to inform him of the note. She told him, "I don't want anybody else to see this note before you get it. I won't disclose the contents to anyone as I am sure that is what you would want."

Zack had already been informed of the escape and was concerned by it. The news from Julia added fear for Rose's safety to his worries. He called the office at the college to alert security about the situation. He asked that they remain vigilant, and to caution Rose to do the same. Zack requested they ask Rose to call home as soon as she could. He would wait by the phone for her call.

The police were visited by a frantic driver who informed them he had picked up a prison guard who had claimed his squad car broke down. The guard told him that he was taking a prisoner to see her father who was on his deathbed, and needed to get to Highway 9, where they were to be picked up by a State Trooper. They needed to get there fast because they were running behind schedule and did not want to miss their connection. Once they reached Highway 9, the driver offered to let them wait in his car until their intended ride arrived. Without pause, they told him it would not be necessary because they only had six minutes to wait until the arranged meeting time. The guard was very polite and very caring for the young lady who was visibly shaken by the whole ordeal.

"What time was it that you picked the couple up?" questioned the officer. "And did the guard have any weapons in his possession?"

"It must have been about 6:30 a.m. As far as weapons are concerned, I really did not notice, I was not looking for them. I had an 8:00 a.m. appointment to do an assessment on a farm that is for sale. My intent was to be there by 7:30 a.m. in order to meet the real estate agent who is selling the property. No one is living there so he had to unlock the premises for me to get my job done."

The policeman told him, "You can consider yourself a lucky man. The little angel that was so upset is a fugitive from a possible attempted murder charge. She is also wanted for kidnapping and will now have a fugitive from justice charge added to the list. There is concern that she has intentions to finish what she has started. We have to get her before she is able to accomplish that."

After dismissing the witness, the officer immediately radioed the information he gathered and concentrated on the last known whereabouts of the fugitives. He surmised that they were holed up in the Appalachian Foothills, or possibly in the State of Alabama by now. A check was being made to determine if either of the two might have relatives in the vicinity that would offer them safe harbor.

It seemed that everyone in Europa had become aware of the situation and Julia's café was buzzing with conversation. To the best of Julia's knowledge, the contents of the note had not been made public information. The one thing to be avoided was to have

Rose become aware of what they were. It was enough for her to bear the news of Chantele's escape.

In addition to the news of Chantele's escape, the news of the economy became bleaker by the day. The public had been feeling the effects of the slowing economy since mid-year 1929. It had certainly had an effect on the business dealings of Zack and the family. In September of 1929, the Stock Market crashed, creating banking panic and causing many banks to fail. Loans were hard to secure, interest rates were high, and unemployment was on the rise. The predictions regarding a recovery were dire, and some economists were concerned that it possibly would not come for at least ten years.

Everyone was affected by the market crash. People who lost fortunes were committing suicide, businesses were closing, and repossessions were rampant. Many people suffered from the lack of food and were starving. Bread and soup lines were formed to help feed the destitute. Many religious and charitable organizations were doing all they could to help the needy. Zack's concerns had just intensified and weighed heavily on his mind.

A week went by when Elmo, who was busy in the stable, heard a car drive onto the property. He saw a gentleman and young woman get out of the car and start their way up to the stable area. He became aware of a noticeable limp in the gait of the young lady who accompanied the man. He realized it was Mr. Branson, the owner of the horse Rusty, and his daughter. They went through the normal formalities, and Branson told Elmo they would like to see Sally.

Elmo brought her out and proceeded to lead her around a bit when Mr. Branson's daughter, Jeannie, asked if she might lead her. Elmo turned the lead rope over to her and both of them slowly walked around the area. She took the lead rope and looped it around the back of Sally's neck. She then walked slowly in front of her. Sally quickly obliged her and started to walk just behind her. She was well pleased with the process and presented a beaming smile of approval. She felt that Sally was aware of the fact that they both had a leg problem. It was her thought that they were made for each other.

Elmo suggested, "You should have your vet check Sally out before any decisions are made. I do want you to know that Robbie has not been made aware of the possibility of this trade. He will ultimately decide if there is or is not to be a deal."

Mr. Branson replied, "I don't need any further check of Sally. My vet, who also happens to be Bart Sloan, has advised me of her present state of health and his opinion regarding her future well-being. I am confident that I would be trading for a sound and wonderful horse for my daughter to ride. I am also aware that it is for Robbie to make the final decision. I am confident that he, although it will be difficult for him to do so, will choose in favor of letting my daughter have Sally. I hope that I'll hear from you soon regarding his decision. We thank you for your interest in the matter, and bid you farewell. I'll be waiting for your response."

Over at the Colonel's farm, activity had picked up considerably. More people were coming, and people that he had not seen before were arriving to get free vegetables. The effects of the depression started to cause concern for him, and he wondered how he would be able to help all of the people. He didn't have the answer to the question, but he knew he had a problem. He would have to come up with an answer soon and would need to turn to someone for help.

The call that came in from the Sheriff's office was not to Zack's liking. They had not been able to locate the two fugitives, and they had no idea where they could possibly have gone.

What the law officers were not aware of was that the two fugitives were hiding in the vacated farmhouse the assessor spoke of on the first leg of their escape. It's where they decided to lay low while the search remained in high alert mode. Chantele was in an unusually tranquil mood and relied on her accomplice to determine the strategy at this point. After a week of successfully evading capture and remaining undetected, the search slowed down. It appeared safe for them to move out after dark and go by way of lightly traveled country roads. They planned to flag down a passing vehicle and subdue a lone driver.

Chantele applied a tourniquet to her left arm, and used a long branch fashioned into a walking stick to fake an injury. They had been on a very deserted road for several hours and there was not a single sign of a vehicle.

She hastened to tell Rogers, "You sure made a lousy choice selecting this road as our way out of here."

He replied, "You didn't object to this route when we started out. You do know we have to avoid the law, especially while they may still be searching for us in this area. I am not of the mind to be caught and be put behind bars."

Chantele hesitantly blurted out, "I was just saying. I have no intentions of being penned up again either. I just wish we were in Alabama. I would feel a lot better in the security of my dumb cousin's house. You are in for a surprise when you meet him. One good thing is that he will give you the shirt off his back. You won't even have to ask for it. Hey, look there's an old truck coming this way, we are in luck."

Rogers cautioned her, "Don't say a word, I'll do the talking. If you are asked a question directly about our destination, tell him it's Everglades City in Florida. Make sure you keep giving the same answer to any question you may have been previously asked. When in doubt about what to say, tell him my husband makes those decisions. Tell him that makes for a happy marriage. Put on your, 'I am hurting act.' Remember, we don't know anybody near here and that is why getting to Everglades City is so important to us. Should he be questioned by the Sheriff about us, he'll be sure to mention something about our destination. They'll be looking for us where we are not."

The truck came to a grinding stop. The noise coming from the engine sounded like a passel of squealing hogs. The driver, although very friendly, was not somebody you wanted to get up close and personal with. He had a Rip Van Winkle look about him, along with a Bathless Groggins habit. The twinkle in his eyes may have been a result of some imbibing he had done. The empty bottle bearing the Buffalo Trace label confirmed the fact that he had recently taken a few too many swigs.

After giving them a thorough once-over, he bellowed out, "Great gobs of goose grease. Little missy what happened to the train that hit you?" He let out a guffaw that could be heard in the next county over. His last comment apparently amused him. "The jokes are over, we got to find you some medical help."

Rogers informed him that she had seen a doctor and told him, "What she needs is to get off her feet. She needs rest and a ride would provide a lot of help. Where are you headed for?" Going anywhere in the direction of Alabama was suitable for them. "Could you possibly give us a ride? We are heading for Everglade City in Florida, and you can drop us off at the Alabama border where we can pick up a ride heading to Florida."

"I'll be glad to help," he earnestly stated, "and I want you to know that I am glad I came across a nice young couple like you two."

It was about a three-hour ride, which seemed like five to a pair of desperados breathing in the unpleasant air of the rundown truck. Chantele insisted on having the window seat. She couldn't handle being in the middle.

They reached an agreement that Rip was not a threat to them. Rogers said, "He won't remember anything if he is to be questioned by the police. We can let him go on his way. We certainly don't want his old wreck anyhow. The jalopy sputters, squeals, and stinks. It could die on us tomorrow."

The parting was short and sweet. Rip told them, "I'll never forget you two, catch you later," and waved goodbye to them.

Chantele warily said, "I really don't feel good at all about his parting statement. Let's hope we were not too hasty in our judgement and didn't underestimate the man."

Chapter 14:
Parting Brings Much Sorrow

Three days had passed since Mr. Branson and his daughter visited, and there was still no decision from Robbie. Zack was growing impatient with his failure to do so and intended to act. He thought it was rude to keep them waiting for an answer, and he wanted one also.

Elmo and Robbie were in the kitchen having a cup of coffee and discussing the trade matter when Zack came into the house. He joined them and at once, was brought into the conversation by Elmo. "Son, I have been telling Robbie the reasons it is to our benefit to trade Sally. I mentioned the fact that she will never race again, might have trouble with the breeding process, and might possibly require more care and attention. We sure don't have extra time to devote to that care, if needed, as we have our hands full at the present."

Zack responded in agreement and added, "We are also going to need to increase our soybean production because of lagging sales of other products, which will demand even more of our time. We all know the money situation is growing tighter, so any new acquisitions will have to be secured on a bartering basis until we have cash to make further purchases. Robbie, I know you are attached to Sally, but Rusty drew your attention for a reason. I suspect he will be a horse that you will enter into races. I believe he will become a noticeable attraction 'standing at stud' and could possibly bring a higher rate for his service. The potential for adding more revenue is of great importance to us right now."

Robbie sadly replied, "I wasn't looking at the big picture, which I should have all along. My biggest incentive for parting with her would be to help a young lady in search of a fitting horse to satisfy her needs. It's not easy for me to say yes, but when I consider the enjoyment she will derive from owning Sally, I find it even harder to say no. It's a done deal. Why don't you call the Bransons and tell them the news? This looks to be a win-win situation for everybody."

"Now for some not so good news," Zack noted. "The last call from Rose brought some disturbing news. She received a note from Chantele warning her not to get too comfortable, and to know there is a score needing to be settled. I don't know yet what will be required of me. The Sheriff said they haven't been able to determine where they might be located, or where they may be headed. On another note, I also had a talk with Colonel Burns, who is concerned he will be unable to continue his vegetable give-away program for much longer. He doesn't know where to turn for help, and I suggested that we might be able to lend some support. We have to put our heads together and figure out a way to help him."

Current circumstances did not leave any time to figure out how to help Colonel Burns. He was on the way to the hospital in an ambulance suffering from difficulty breathing. As soon as the call from the Colonel's neighbor was received, Zack and Elmo left for the hospital. Upon arrival, they were quickly greeted by a nurse who said the surgeon required a signature from Zack in order to perform surgery. Colonel Burns, having no family members, had designated Zack as the contact person should such a need arise.

Within a short period of time, who appeared to be the attending surgeon, approached Zack and Elmo. They were apprehensive over what they anticipated to be bad news. The doctor allayed their fears but did tell them that the situation was not good. Two bullets that had been lodged near his lungs were causing his breathing difficulties and it was too dangerous to try to remove them. This was probably determined to be the case at the time he was wounded.

The doctor went on to say, "Bed rest and administered oxygen will be the answer to his needs at this time. We will have to see how he responds to the treatment before determining next steps. He will be bed ridden for a period of time. I will stay in touch with you."

The need for an answer as to how to provide help came much too soon.

Zack was puzzled. "He never did mention the fact he was wounded in all the time since we have known him. I do believe he is a man of many secrets. I'll tell him we will tend to the horses. It will be nice to be around Smoky again. Bob should also know we will keep his giveaway program intact and that he should not worry. I have no idea how we are going to manage all of this, but we will figure something out in a big hurry. Remember, we also need to go to the trial tomorrow at the County Courthouse. I sure wish it were Chantele along with Max who was facing trial. It would surely ease my mind."

"Zack," Elmo added, "We can handle the situation. You have two exceptionally fine young ones that will pitch in and do anything asked of them. I am ready to take on more work, and I can handle the Colonel's property by myself. Robbie will have to take on a little more of my chores, although I don't like the idea of it interfering with his schooling. I'm sure that Camelia will not mind getting her hands dirty. She can tend to the feeding of the horses and clean the stalls. Together, this family of ours can handle anything thrown our way."

As they entered the courtroom, Zack was astounded by what he saw. "Dad, will you get a load of Otto? He's dressed in his Sunday go-to-church clothes. I am not used to seeing him so spruced up. I guess that I shouldn't be surprised since I have never been to any function with him that required the need for formal dress. I sure wonder what's going through his mind right now."

Elmo responded, "He seems to be bearing up well given the circumstances. I can only assume he's not happy about being here, and I'm sure he will be called to offer testimony."

The Judge came out of his Chambers, and the "All Rise" was called out and quickly responded to by all present in the Courtroom. The bailiff announced, "The Court with the Honorable Judge Morton is in session. Please be seated and come to order."

The trial began with several witnesses called to testify for the prosecution. Max sat quietly with his attorney and appeared to be in a pensive mood as Miss Rose Barrow was called to take the stand. She was advised that she was under oath and swore on The Bible to tell the truth in the matter.

The prosecutor posed several questions. "Miss Barrow, were you held against your will?" Rose responded in the affirmative.

"Were you blocked from leaving?

She answered, "Yes."

"Were you bound in any manner?"

"I was locked in a bathroom until my grandpa freed me."

The prosecutor indicated that there was no need for further questioning, and Rose was excused.

The prosecutor then called Mr. Robbie Barrow to the stand. He questioned Robbie as to why he was at the Schwartz residence. "I was there to see if my sister was in any danger," he explained.

"And was she?"

"Upon entering the house, we found her locked in a bathroom."

"No further questions. You may be excused," the prosecutor announced.

The attorney for the defense then called Miss Rose Barrow to the witness stand. "Miss Barrow, at any time did you feel your life was in danger?"

"Yes, I did."

"Did anything happen to give you any hope?

"Yes, Mr. Brunner arranged for me to escape." Rose gave testimony to the fact that she knew that Mr. Brunner was an unwilling accomplice and had heard Chantele warn him that he was a partner to her actions. Rose was then excused and returned to her seat in the courtroom.

The defense called their final witnesses to take the stand, the last of whom was Otto Schwartz. Otto presented his testimony, and stated, "Max was duped by a Jezebel. I overheard conversations between him and Chantele, and she was in total command of the situation. He pleaded with her not to carry out her plans and wanted no part in it. I do not have any malice towards Max, since, in my view, he had done nothing wrong. His mistake was getting involved with a woman who is on a vendetta to do harm to an innocent young lady. He did everything he could to arrange a means for Miss Barrow to escape. He wanted no part in the matter."

The courtroom erupted with an outburst of disbelief at what happened. Everyone was astounded and could not believe that he came to the defense of someone who poisoned him.

No additional testimony followed, and the Judge announced that he was ready to present judgement. "After hearing the testimony of Miss Barrow and Mr. Schwartz, and there being no evidence presented that implicates Mr. Brunner in a kidnapping, I find the defendant Maximillian Brunner guilty of being an accomplice in a lesser charge, the false imprisonment of Miss Barrow. I am not ruling for a jail sentence for your complicity in the matter, but I do rule for probation for a term of three years from this date. Please be aware, Mr. Brunner, that if you violate the terms of your probation, you will be subject to immediate arrest."

The judge announced, "Court is adjourned."

All parties were satisfied with the terms set forth and exited the courtroom. There was absolute amazement at the turn the trial had taken, and most agreed that justice had been carried out in the case.

Chapter 15:
A Compassionate Trade

Grandpa called out to Robbie, "Do you want to see Sally off before I take her over to the Branson's farm?"

"You know, I have been visiting with her these last few days, and I thought it would be best if I do not do so on her last day here," replied Robbie. "I have gotten much too attached to her and it will be hard to see her leave."

Robbie went on telling Grandpa, "I love horses, love being around them, and I want to become the best breeder I can be."

"Oh," Grandpa answered, "you are on your way to becoming just that. I have watched you, and tried to teach you what little I might know. It is apparent to me that you are on the right track. If you have the desire and will to dream, and the capacity to work, you can achieve anything you set your mind to do. I do want you to understand this fact. You can dream all the dreams in the world, but without hard work they will be fruitless. Anything worth achieving requires due diligence. Reach for the stars, Robbie. Be the best you can be in whatever you pursue."

"Something else I just recently learned from my son, your father," Elmo went on to say, "is that there are times in life when sentimentality has to be tempered and personal desires require denial. The well-being of, in our case, family and business, has to be number one priority. My attachment to Smoky, and yours to Sally, furthered our selfish desires. We were not thinking about the real needs of our family and business. The present economic condition in our country demands that we are thoughtful in our decisions and frugal when it comes to satisfying our appetites."

As Elmo sorrowfully loaded Sally onto the trailer for the trip, Robbie came by, slapped her on her rump, and continued on without stopping. It was a gloomy and cool day with a strong prevailing wind, adding to the despondency of the proceedings. Elmo finished loading her onto the trailer and set off for her new destination.

The Branson clan must have been waiting eagerly for Sally, as the whole family was already gathered outside. Young Miss Jeannie was thrilled and delighted upon the arrival of Elmo, who was bringing her anticipated treasure. She started to dart out to greet the expected visitor, when her father gently held her back.

Sally was unloaded and emitted a loud nicker, almost to say, "I'm glad to be here." When Jeannie approached her, Sally immediately placed her muzzle onto her face. It was a sight to behold and brought much satisfaction and confirmation to Elmo that it was the right decision they had made.

He wasted no time getting Rusty onto the trailer and soon headed back in the direction of Happy Acres Farm. He had a good feeling about the trade and felt that both parties were dealt a fair deal. Benefits of the trade would be enjoyed by each of them.

Back at the farm, while unloading Rusty, Elmo took a different view of the trade. He told Robbie, "We are the lucky ones. We definitely got the better end of the deal."

"I hope the Branson family feels the same way about the transaction." Robbie responded.

Robbie watched as their new horse was unloaded and was surprised at the interaction between Rusty and Grandpa. It was as if they had been together for a long time. He continued to watch what he determined to be a mutual admiration event. He was glad for Elmo, who now had Rusty to replace Smoky, and happy he now had Sparky to take the place of Sally. He found it easy to see why those connections were made, when in fact there were fourteen other horses on the farm. He could now give more attention to the beautiful colt born on that tar-black stormy night.

Chapter 16:
Continued Threats

Thanksgiving Day was drawing near, and excitement built up inside of Rose. She contemplated her first visit back to the farm, being home, visiting, and playing Grandpa's Game with the whole family present. Visions of roast turkey, mom's delicious stuffing, along with her mashed potatoes, candied yams, and cranberry sauce filled her thoughts. What excited her most was being with family.

Rose weathered the fitful threats that she continued to receive. She had not allowed fear to dominate her existence. She felt relatively safe at school and was further comforted by the fact that shy Denny, the quiet one, notified her he was keeping a watch out for any suspicious activity he might notice.

All went very well academically for her, and she was in love with the school, its professors, and the school's values. The culture and the climate promoted a secure and wholesome learning environment. She gained a share of notoriety due to the predicament that permeated her life and threatened her security.

Her thoughts reflected her desire. *Thanksgiving, hurry up and get here. I want the love and kindness that are ever present in my home.*

All was going rather well, both at the farm, and also at Colonel Burns' farm. They were all quite surprised and pleased by how well everything seemed to be working out. The vegetable giveaway had not missed a beat in being able to supply much wanted and sought after food for those in need. Camelia had been a trooper, and the stalls seemed to be neater and cleaner with her in charge of the responsibility. She told her grandpa, "This place was in much need of a woman's touch." That comment brought some well-deserved laughter from the men in the family.

With the last of the sweet potatoes, squash and cucumbers showing signs of being depleted, Grandpa started to put out freshly laid eggs to keep supplying some help to the poverty-stricken food seekers. He put up some chicken wire forming an enclosure he had chosen and placed a group of hatchlings within. It was not long before these little peepers started to lay the precious eggs, so desperately needed, to replace the soon to be unavailable vegetables. He continued to add to the flock in hopes of increasing the supply of eggs.

On several occasions upon returning to the pen area, he noticed things were out of order. He began to determine that the flock was decreasing instead of increasing, and after a week, decided to do some detective work.

One early morning, he asked Robbie to take him to the Colonel's farm. Upon arrival, Robbie was advised to proceed to a designated area where he would be able to intercept the thief. Elmo sought a place in the barn where he could observe unwelcome activity. An alarm sent out by the disturbed chickens alerted him and he noticed a man grabbing chickens and stuffing them in a burlap sack. He shouted out, "Hey you, you're under arrest," causing the man to flee with a bunch of cackling chickens in his sack. The road leading to and from the farm offered an easterly or a westerly direction. It was fortunate that where Robbie had been directed to wait was the direction the thief had taken in his attempt to escape.

As the man drove by, Robbie waited a few seconds and then followed the fleeing chicken bandit to his home. He waited as the man placed the chickens in a little shed and then continued on into his house. Robbie circled back, picked up Elmo, and proceeded to the Police Station. They alerted the officer and followed the squad car to the guilty party's house.

The officer knocked on the door but received no answer. He then called out in a loud voice informing the owner that he was aware of his presence in the house, and that a warrant had been issued to search the premises. This action earned the attention of the occupants in the house, and a lady came to the door asking, "What is the problem officer?"

In reply, the officer said, "It's about a case of stolen chickens from the property of Colonel Robert Burns."

With a puzzled look, she asked, "Why are you coming to our house regarding that matter?"

Officer Jones told her, "Because a man was trailed back to this house after grabbing some chickens and putting them in a burlap sack. The fact is those chickens are in your shed, I can hear them clucking from where I stand."

"Oh!" she stated, "My husband has permission to get chickens there and pass them on to needy people. Why, just yesterday Colonel Burns told him he could continue to do so."

Officer Jones wanted to know, "Just exactly where was he when he spoke to Colonel Burns?"

"My husband was given permission while he was at the Colonel's home."

The officer then told her, "Your husband is not being truthful with you, ma'am, and I am here to collect the evidence and to place him under arrest for thievery. Tell your husband to come out of hiding, or I will call in more officers. If he should refuse, we will take him by force. That will add resisting arrest to his charges."

The husband reluctantly obeyed and came out of hiding, was handcuffed, and placed into the patrol car for the trip to the jail.

He was heard mumbling, "This is the thanks that I get for trying to help the poor?"

After hearing the man's remark, Elmo told the Police Officer, "I don't intend to press charges since his motive was to help hungry people."

The officer responded, "I assure you his actions were in no way a charitable act. We have had complaints from several sources claiming that they had been approached by someone selling chickens. When they refused to buy from him, he got very nasty with them. This guy is a snake in the woodpile. We will have enough evidence, along with those witnesses, to charge him. I despise a person that would perpetrate something like this."

"If he in fact did as you say, to let him go scot-free from these sorts of actions would only embolden him to continue. It is sad that this sort of thing happens. I, for one, want peace and security, and freedom from fear, which will not be available to us unless law is meted out fairly and swiftly to all offenders."

"That is what we all want and what we all deserve. Elmo, you have not seen what I have seen or heard what I have heard from the law enforcement officials in some of our cities. Without law and order, the cities would become jungles."

Chapter 17:
Much to Be Thankful For

Thanksgiving finally arrived, and Rose happily assisted Tessie with the meal preparations. It was a brisk and frosty morning they awoke to this day. Elmo, Zack, and Robbie were out doing the necessary chores. After all, the animals needed to be tended to. Work had no holiday on the farm. Elmo needed to scoot over to the Colonel's to feed and water the horses, throw out some chicken feed for the ravenous flock, and make sure all was right with everything.

Having completed all that needed to be taken care of, they all sat down for breakfast and gave thanks for the first meal of the day. One by one they recited what they had to be thankful for in their life. As the conversation passed from one to the other, it became apparent that Rose's safety was at the forefront of everyone's mind. They all cited her safety as of paramount concern while expressing gratitude for her well-being.

The chatter continued for a long while and centered fairly well around Colonel Burns' condition. Zack reassured the family when he said, "I stay in touch with Dr. Morgan on a daily basis and it seems that he is well pleased with the Colonel's progress thus far. He feels that physical exertion coupled with anxiety about his food give-away program triggered his problem. He thinks another week of hospital confinement is just the medicine he needs right now. The Colonel will not be able to perform physical labor of any sort until Dr. Morgan releases him for light activity, but I am pleased with what I heard about his present state of health, and I have a good feeling regarding his recovery."

"Dad, I know that Colonel Bob is very happy about the egg program that you have started, and he is wondering if you can think of anything else we can do."

Tessie chimed in saying, "We ladies have a lot of kitchen work to perform, and if you want to enjoy our usually great meal, we have got to get to work."

"Aye, aye, Captain," Elmo laughingly exclaimed. Breakfast came to a happy end, and everyone looked forward to Tessie's promise of a great meal.

A food seeker over at Colonel Burn's farm called Elmo to tell him a fox was seen up by the chicken enclosure. He related, "I am next door calling from the neighbor's phone. I do not hear any alarm signs, but I think it might be advisable for you to come over and be prepared to dispatch him if necessary."

"Thank you so much. Zack and I are on the way over, we're leaving right now."

When they arrived the fox was gone, but signs of his being there were very visible. Elmo softly muttered, "Well, there will be less eggs for the needy now. I'm not going to be able to be here all the time to stand guard over them."

Zack tendered some advice, "No you can't be here all the time, but we can have Rollo here to do the guarding. He will keep skunks, and the sneaky fox critters away. He might even keep the hawks from attempting to swoop in. There is always an answer to a problem. It's a good thing that Rex came along with Rusty in that swap we had made with the Branson family. Rex can guard our property, while Rollo takes care of the Colonel's. Let's be thankful the fox did not kill anymore chickens than he did. We should head back to the house and enjoy the company of our wonderful family."

Dinner was exactly what Tessie said it would be, perfect as ever. There were a few things missing from the traditional dinner, necessitated by the undesirable depression they were experiencing. They were fortunate to be able to live off the land for the most part. There was not a lot of food they had to purchase to stave off hunger.

"I hope the Colonel and the others at the hospital were able to enjoy a fine meal today." Zack was heard saying.

Tessie added, "I was not able to make our customary pies, but I did make some bread pudding. I intend to take some over to the Colonel later. I would like it if we all would go together and brighten up his day. We can even do it now, what do you say?" A chorus of "I'll go" rang out in unison, they quickly boarded the car for the visit.

The Colonel was found sitting in the sunroom taking advantage of the bright sunlight beaming into the room. He was surprised as he spotted the welcome sight of the Barrow clan making their way towards him. A broad smile graced his appealing countenance, and he was full of joy upon greeting them. He was also full of questions. "How is everybody? Rose, how are things going at school? Are there any problems at my place I should be aware of?"

They came bounding out a mile a minute, leaving no time for an answer for any one of them. He apologized and added, "I'm getting ahead of myself. I will slow down so we can all talk. I am so glad you are here with me. It means so much."

Answers came to all his questions, along with questions being asked of him.

Rose spoke first. "I am so happy to see you, and glad to hear the good news Dr. Morgan had to say about your speedy recovery. Do you have any idea when they are going to release you from the hospital? I have been genuinely concerned about your predicament and I continue praying for your recovery."

"My dear Rose, it is your safety that is a cause for worry for all of us. Not a day goes by that I find myself in total disbelief about what has transpired. You are on my mind, and I pray that you remain vigilant and stay safe."

Elmo wanted to know, "How did you get the news about the egg program? I was reluctant to say anything about it for fear it would cause you to worry."

"Worry, not at all. I was so happy you came up with the idea. I found out from an elderly lady who benefits from the program. She came to see me here and could not restrain herself from thanking me for my generosity. I was a bit embarrassed when she kept on and on about the matter. I hope that you might figure out other items we could offer to help everybody in these desperate times. Make sure to keep track of your expenses as I intend to repay you for whatever is owed."

More questions and answers ensued, and it became apparent that the Colonel seemed to be tiring. Time passed and Elmo wanted to get home in time for a round of Grandpa's Game. He always had a concern about how time was slipping away. They bid farewells and bounded off for a night ending game of cards.

It was not a minute after they entered the house that Grandpa reached into the drawer for the playing cards. They all paid heed to the fact that he expected them to sit down and get the show on the road. There was no time to waste when it came to playing his favorite game.

Midway through the game, with Elmo in the lead, Camelia was prompted to ask, "Does being the scorekeeper have anything to do with the fact you have the highest score?"

Robbie replied, "It could be he is stacking the cards."

Grandpa offered some sage advice. "Maybe it is because I am the best player at the table. Did any of you consider that fact?"

Whatever the reason for his success in the game, he was found to be the highest scoring player as they completed the last hand of the game. As luck would have it, the game, even though highly contested by Camelia, ended up with another victory for the unbeatable Elmo.

Zack asked the question, "Why do we even play when we get the same results so often?"

Camelia added, "I guess in order to humor Grandpa."

He smiled and retorted, "Losers."

It was an evening filled with fun, caring, and sharing of each other's love that came to an end. "Good night, sleep tight," was passed back and forth between the family.

"You are going to be treated with leftovers for the next couple of days," rang out from Tessie as she cleaned up the remnants of the snacks they had been enjoying. "Good night now."

Chapter 18:
Seeking Safe Harbor

The morning after began with the men completing the necessary chores and the two girls preparing breakfast in the kitchen with their mother. The aromas wafting from their cooking brought thoughts of joy, peace, and comfort to Rose, along with feelings of reluctance to leave what offered her such contentment. She shifted her thoughts to being back for Christmas and resigned herself to accepting the fact that she had to return to school on Sunday. At this moment she was going to enjoy the pleasure of the visit and love every minute of it.

Breakfast was served. Homemade biscuits, bacon from Mr. Brown, honey from Harry Sparks, and eggs from the Devlin farm. It was helpful that Zack was able to trade his vegetables for the fresh makings of this morning's meal. The dwindling supply of this year's potatoes were used to provide the delicious hash browns everyone so enjoyed.

Reminiscing took up a good part of the morning's conversation and allowed for some good memories along with a whole lot of laughter. Grandpa recollected a serious but funny situation. "I can't forget the day I was cleaning the septic tank in the outbuilding. I removed the manhole cover preparing to add some chemicals to the system. Robbie came bouncing over, and I warned him to be careful because he could fall into the tank. No sooner than I said that he slipped right in. He certainly was not going into the house to get cleaned up and I was not getting too close to him either. Once he was out, I turned the garden hose on him. I was able to get the waste off of him, but it took a lot more than water from the hose to get the stench off of him. He was called "Little Stinky" for quite some time. He never did go near there again."

The stories continued for a good while, until someone suggested they all take a ride over to the Colonel's farm to check things out. There was not a car to be seen on the roads as they motored to his farm. The Thanksgiving dinners the townspeople ate yesterday must have tired everybody out.

Everyone was anxious to see Smoky and headed directly to his stall. He apparently felt the same way about seeing them and let out some loud whinnies and nickers. He stomped the ground repeatedly. He wanted the family to know he had not forgotten them. They spent a good part of an hour visiting and brushing and stroking him. All was well with the other horses. They refreshed their water and added a small bit of feed to carry them over until the morning. The Barrows thought on feeding of their horses was to feed little and feed often and feed the same time every day. Satisfied that all was well, they were back on the road heading toward home.

It was a different scene at the home of Cousin Rafe in Alabama. Chantele was still complaining about the Thanksgiving Day meal. "Why aren't you raising turkeys? We wouldn't have had to eat stinking gamey venison yesterday. I don't believe your father taught you anything. I was hoping for a good meal, not Salvation Army food. When I asked for a drink of whiskey, what did I get? Rotten tasting moonshine. It's a wonder I am still living and breathing this morning."

Rafe sheepishly answered, "It might have been more peaceful here if you were not. My day is already starting out bad."

Chantele wanted to know, "Do you talk rudely to all your guests? It appears that your folks forgot to teach you manners. Well, what are we going to do today?"

Rafe answered, "You'll probably lay in bed all day and smoke like you have since arriving here. After the rest of us clean up the place, I am going hunting in hopes of bagging another nice Buck. That way I can have a lot more stinking gamey venison to eat. I wasn't born with a silver spoon in my mouth like you were. It sure is no wonder to me why your father wanted you out of his house. You need to start thinking about getting on the road. There is an end to the charity coming soon. Real soon."

With the house cleaned and in order, Rafe grabbed his hunting rifle and went on his way to a peaceful and tranquil day in the woods.

After he left, Chantele admonished Rogers. "What kind of man are you, allowing that stupid cousin of mine to talk to me that way? I thought that I had linked up with someone who would stand up for me. You heard what the nerd said, what do you have planned?"

Rogers softly answered, "I would guess we should be packing up what little we have and get on the road. You didn't exactly endear yourself to him."

"That's quite a stupid plan, and I don't want to hear any more insulting remarks from you. I don't intend on leaving here empty handed."

"Well, what exactly do you have in mind?" Rogers asked. "I don't intend to be a party to stealing or causing harm to anybody. I believed you when you told me that Maximillian made the plans and administered the poison to his boss. Now, I am beginning to think it was all you and am wondering if I can believe anything you say. I for one am ready to leave. Are you coming with me?"

"Have a nice walk alone, Rogers. I am taking Rafe's car and getting out of this rathole. Goodbye, goody two shoes. I don't suppose you will ever man up. I find it refreshing to part from a loser."

Rafe returned from his unsuccessful hunt in the woods, lacking the prized Buck he had anticipated bagging. Rogers, who was seated at the kitchen table, unfolded the tale. "Your loving cousin has run off on me. She didn't leave empty handed though. She is now driving your automobile to who knows where."

"Wow, what a real piece of work. How in the world did you get hooked up with her?"

Rogers relayed the story to him, and asked, "When you call the police to notify them of your stolen vehicle, would you tell them that a prison escapee is here, and wants to turn himself in?"

The police arrived, gathered pertinent information from Rafe, and took their escaped criminal into custody.

The police questioned Rogers about Chantele's potential whereabouts. "Do you have any idea where she might be headed?"

"I wish I knew. But I would certainly like to see her end up behind bars again though," Rafe admitted.

Rogers shared, "I know she has not gone to Florida. That was information given to throw the law off course. She may very well be headed back to Mississippi to settle a vendetta she has cooked up in her evil mind."

The officers thanked Rogers for sharing this information and wondered how in the world he had managed to get himself into this kettle of fish?

Chapter 19:
Justice Is Swift and Fair

At 2:00 a.m. Rafe was awakened by a knock on his door, and the barking of his dog. A police officer greeted a sleepy disheveled Rafe who inquired, "What's going on?"

The officer responded, "We have reason to believe that you are harboring a woman who is a fugitive from justice. An old gent stopped at our station six days ago. He told us he picked up a couple who he suspected were up to no good. He felt like he was lucky to depart from them unharmed. We didn't give much credence to his information due to his unsightly appearance and lack of hygiene."

"Do you mind if we come in and have a look around?"

"Not at all. Like I told the police who were here this afternoon, I had no idea the woman, who is a cousin of mine, was evading the law. She has fled the coop along with my car."

"Where is her male counterpart that escaped prison with her?"

"The police who came to get information about my stolen vehicle took the young man in to custody. He had me call to inform them he wanted to surrender himself and face justice."

The Officer responded, "I wish we had taken the old gent seriously. He said that he overheard her tell the male she had a relative nearby. When we checked to see if that were the case, we realized he could have been right. Not much urgency was assigned to the information he gave us. We could have her in our custody right now if we had followed-up sooner."

Chantele had a knack for making bad moves. Believing Old Rip was not alert enough to trip them up was not the first, nor would it probably be her last miscue. She was on the lam now all by herself and the police were searching for her in a stolen car.

Rogers was taken back to prison. After two weeks in custody, he stood and waited for the Judge's verdict.

"Mr. Rogers," he stated, "after much thought I have arrived at my decision. I want you to think of the gravity of your actions. You have aided a dangerous person to escape, who is now roaming the streets, and now able to inflict harm on an innocent person. You have deprived her intended victim of peace of mind due to the ever-present threat of harm. You, who was serving as a public servant, a prison guard, makes this an even more intolerable act. Your father, an honorable man who retired as a Lieutenant on the Police Force cannot be happy with your misconduct. It is because of him and your other family members, all good citizens, that I feel compelled to offer leniency in your case. I hereby sentence you to four years imprisonment, followed by three years of probation. It is my hope that you will be rehabilitated and make something out of your life once your sentence has been served. I wish the best to you and offer solace to your parents and siblings."

Chapter 20:
Depression Demands

Like Grandpa would say, time kept slipping away. Christmas had come and gone, and Rose was home for a two-week break from her studies. There were fewer gifts under the tree, and the church service was very subdued.

Back at school, the effects of the depression were ever-present. Things were taking a turn for the worse, and people were suffering. The serving portions at the cafeteria were getting smaller, and lights were ordered to be off by 9:30 p.m. each evening. The thermostats were lowered in the dorms, and the temperature in the rooms was less comfortable than normal.

She was not spared from the frightening notes from her nemesis, which she shared with her self-appointed guard Denny. They seemed to be taking on a more ominous tone with each new message. The last one received read:

I SEE THE BODY OF A FEMALE LYING IN A WATER FILLED DRAINAGE DITCH. DO YOU THINK THAT MAY BE THE WAY IT ENDS FOR YOU?

The notes had an unnerving effect on Rose, noticeable to Denny, who reassured her that he would keep a watchful eye out for any sign of trouble. Unbeknownst to Rose, another guardian angel had committed himself to the task, and was of a strong purpose to help out.

Spring brought increased work to everyone at the farm including soil preparation, seed sowing, fertilizing, and keeping the new crops properly watered. They had a respite from these activities for the last four and a half months while they repaired and mended various projects in addition to caring for the animals. With the additional work required of Elmo and Robbie at the Colonel's, the workload was becoming insurmountable. The notion that the Barrows could handle anything handed to them would soon be put to the test.

One thing was sure, they sorely needed the extra money that the increased soybean crop would bring them. The cost of hay, feed, and farrier services were becoming a burden since the business was not bringing in much revenue from services rendered. Folks just did not have the cash for nonessentials. It was all about keeping food on the table. Thankfully, Tessie was faithful in keeping a substantial supply of fruit and vegetables in the food cellar from her canning activity. A good portion of which had been depleted by sharing with some of their less fortunate neighbors and friends.

Colonel Burns had been released from the hospital. He was in good spirits but not keen on the fact that his activities were extremely limited. It was not at all to his liking, and he wondered how he would cope with this fact. He was aware that he still needed help from Elmo and Robbie but was worried he had put too much on them. It would not be as much of a problem four months from now when Robbie and Camelia were off for summer break. It was this span of time between now and then that was of concern to him.

Maximillian came to his mind as a potential source of help. Max had been faithful in adhering to the tenets of his probation charge thus far. After contacting Mr. Schwartz and Max, they both assured him they were willing to help. Otto would check with the court to see if it were permissible. The Colonel expressed his gratitude and told them, "My need is for Max to care for the horses and the stable area. We will work out a fair salary when it is assured that we are not violating any part of the court order. Would you inform me of your findings as soon as you can, please?" He bid them farewell and let out a sigh of relief as he walked slowly back to his car.

On Thursday morning, Otto called to inform the Colonel of the judge's decision. It was not good news and certainly not what he was expecting to hear. The judge felt that it would not be fair, nor healthy for Colonel Burns to have the responsibility of keeping check on Max. He was sorry to have to make a decision he knew did nothing to help the Colonel solve his predicament. Taking everything into consideration, it was the only solution that in his mind was fair and sound.

The Colonel had felt deep down that he would not get the answer he wanted. He had no idea as to where to turn for a solution to his predicament. His neighbors, being farmers, were engaged in keeping their own farms as productive as they possibly could. The young ones in the family had to help their parents and were not available for hire. He derived no comfort in the quandary he was faced with. The added stress of this problem could only hurt him physically and should be avoided per Dr. Morgan.

A visit by the vet to check on an ailing horse led to what might possibly be an answer to it all. Dr. Sloan, while checking on one of the Colonel's three horses, began to tell him about a recent call he had made to check on an ailing mule. "While Dolly here is ailing from too much to eat, the young man I visited in Maben had a different problem. His mule has colic from eating spoiled wet hay. The old girl was suffering rather badly when I arrived. I recommended that he get his hay from a new source, and he said that he gets what he can afford. I told him that the mule would only get sicker and possibly contract laminitis. That it is extremely painful and would incur extensive vet fees. I didn't charge him for the call, and I gave him ten dollars to purchase some good hay. He needs the mule for farming purposes and cannot afford to lose her. There is not much more help that I can afford to give to him."

The Colonel asked, "What can you tell me about him?"

"Nothing much, it was my first meeting with him. He seemed to be a nice young man; I would guess to be about thirty years in age. He kept the property looking fairly well, considering he is probably short on money. He was not dressed in expensive-looking clothes, but they were clean, and he was well groomed. From an outward appearance, I would say he has done some hard work, and seems to be rather capable."

"Would you consider him to be hirable to do some work around my place?"

"Colonel, I can only offer what I have told you so far. I can't vouch for his honesty or work habits. I know nothing of his past history."

"Dr. Sloan, would you hire him based on what you know?"

"What might compel me to do so would be based on strictly trying to help somebody who seems to be down and out. One would not know if he made the right decision or not, without giving him the chance to prove himself."

"With that being said, I am going to give him a chance. I need help, and it sounds like he can use some help also. Dr. Sloan, I thank you, and I sure do appreciate your assistance in this matter. Where did you say he is living?"

"Over in Maben. It is just down the road a piece. I would not be offering any thanks until you get a chance to observe his work ethic."

Months had passed and Chantele was not thrilled with being on her own. She had nobody to blame for any bad decisions that were made. She decided to call her dearly beloved cousin Rafe, to seek shelter with him once again.

"Rafe, hello this is Chantele. I want to thank you for the use of your car, and to let you know that I am on the way to return it to you. I know that I went about it in the wrong way, but I had to escape from that Rogers guy. I was going to leave you a note to warn you that he wanted me to be a party in doing away with you. I wanted no part of it and could only think of distancing myself from him should he go through with it. You know that I think highly of you and cherish the relationship we share. I do want to apologize for being so short with you. He had me so upset I was not thinking straight."

"Chantele, I think highly of you also. I knew that Rogers was up to something and was the reason I kept my deer rifle close by should he attempt anything. I have a good sixth sense about things like that. I have been worried about you, and I am glad you are alright. I am looking forward to seeing you back here. You're going to have to be the cook. I've burned my hands and need help. I can hardly hold this phone. I have to get off of here. Where are you now so that I can know the time of your arrival?"

"Unless something goes wrong, I should be there late this evening or early morning. Keep the door unlocked so I don't have to wake you. Bye for now, sweetie."

Chantele sighed, hung up the phone, and let out a loud laugh. *How can somebody be so gullible?*

Out of an abundance of caution, she did not intend to arrive for three or four days. Nothing like playing it safe, she thought.

A week went by and still there was no sign of Chantele. Rafe was puzzled by her absence. The police had given up on the surveillance shifts they had been conducting. The lead officer told him, "We are not going to be able to continue with the watches. I believe your cousin has fed you a tale about her intentions. We will make several passes by your place each day. If she happens to come back, put a red scarf on the porch rocker to alert us of her return. That is in case you are not able to make a call with her being present."

Dear cousin Chantele stopped at a remote gas station that handled a small amount of the most needed food products, attended by a young man. On the way into the station, she figured that the clerk, a man by the name of Lonnie, would be easily duped. She approached him and said, "I am so lucky that I was able to make it here before running out of gas. I had a terrible experience today. I stopped to help two men seeking help. When I approached their vehicle, one of them grabbed me and started to force me into the rear of their auto. I got in and exited the other side and ran back to my car. I dropped my purse in my haste to get in my car. He picked up my purse and got back into his car but did not pursue me. I was afraid that they might try to assault me, but apparently, they were not going to continue with that in mind since I escaped from them. They got my purse, and what little money that I had with me. I am frightened to continue on in the event they may come back after me. I have no money for gas, I'm hungry, and totally exhausted from my experience. Can you help me in any way?"

She was correct. He was easily duped, and offered, "Don't you worry, I can fill your tank, and you can stay here with me until I close for the day. I live with my grandparents, and I am sure that they would welcome the opportunity of offering safe lodging to you. You will certainly be welcome to join us at the table for our evening meal. Grandma and grandpa are elderly and would enjoy a young lady's company."

"And how about you, would you enjoy my company?" she coyly asked.

Chantele and her young hero arrived at the house of his grandparents where she was warmly greeted. She was invited to take part in the evening meal, and after they finished eating, she told the grandparents of her awful ordeal. She was genuinely welcome to share a meal with them, but they were wary regarding their grandson's request that she be allowed to stay and share the safety of their house. After much thought into the matter, they finally conceded and agreed to have her stay until she was rested and felt safe to go on.

Each day she presented the notion that she was not sure she would ever overcome the fear that was gripping her. His grandparents felt that she was taking advantage of their hospitality and told the grandson that it was time for her to leave. Each day he begged them for her to be able to stay one more day. Grandma and Grandpa observed the hold she had on their grandson, and it became more than they could bear. Chantele was advised that she must leave the next day. She became upset and wanted to spend the day at the service station with Lonnie.

While at the station, she continued to plead with him to get permission for her to stay longer. "If they say no to your request, I would like for you to come with me."

Lonnie's emotions were tugging at his heart, and he found it hard to answer, "I would love to, but I have to stay and care for my grandparents. I am all that they have, and they need my help."

She was disgusted with his answer. "After all the time we have spent together, is that all you think of me? I prolonged my stay so that we could be together. I wanted to be with you. I would have left the first day after dinner had I known that I would be treated so badly by you. If I were not afraid to leave in the evening, I would go right now. The least you could do for me would be to give me twenty dollars, so I don't have to beg for my next meal."

Chantele left the next morning without saying goodbye or offering thanks for the generous hospitality she enjoyed over the last month. She left with twenty dollars that Lonnie took out of his savings, along with fifty dollars she had stolen while at the station yesterday.

Back at the Colonel's farm, the new guy, Leon, from over at Maben, had worked out nicely since the Colonel hired him two weeks ago. He liked the Colonel and was quite satisfied with the pay arrangement they agreed upon. In addition to the money he received, he would also get fresh eggs and vegetables once the crop was harvested. The only hitch in the matter was that he had to take orders from a youngster who would be returning to school in the fall as a junior in high school.

Now that Robbie and Camelia, along with Tessie were on summer vacation, a good part of the load had been taken off of Elmo and Zack. That fact was a relief to all concerned, especially the Colonel.

Rose had been asked to stay on at school to complete some lab work that she had been assisting a professor with. She received another threatening message the day she was supposed to leave for home. It read: YOU HAVE FINISHED YOUR FIRST YEAR OF COLLEGE. IT MAY TURN OUT TO BE YOUR LAST. With the campus vacated for the summer she felt less secure and was getting somewhat jittery. Denny had stayed on also but would have to leave in two days. That did nothing to soothe her. She would miss his company and wondered if she should leave to get to the safety of her home. It was not easy for her to answer as she had been honored with the laboratory task and felt obligated to complete the experiment.

There was also another reason that she had been asked to stay on, though she did not know why. The president of the college was meeting with the Board to determine some matters concerning next year's operations. They needed to know how they would cope with the effects that the current economic situation had on them. One of the questions had a direct bearing on Rose's future for next year. The president wanted an answer, so that he could speak to Rose directly. The answer was not forthcoming, and she had to leave at the end of the week without knowing the outcome.

Chapter 21:
On the Road Again

The morning Chantele left to continue to her destination was a stormy, gloomy, and somewhat dangerous day to be on the road. She headed into what was predicted to be a tornado. She was unaware of the forecast and was genuinely concerned about the weather picture she was faced with. She really did not know where she needed to go. Should she go back to Cousin Rafe's house, head for Starkville, or end up near Europa? She knew she did not want to be in Europa for fear of being recognized. This fact compelled her to change her look completely while at Lonnie's grandparents' home, telling him she was doing it to please him. It would be hard for anyone to recognize her, even her close associates.

The heavy winds and the blowing rain made visibility difficult and caused her to pull over onto a deserted road for a long while. She was frightened and concerned about her well-being. While doing so, she was buffeted by strong winds which threatened to overturn the car. The sounds of sirens were heard in the distance and drew closer. She was able to see the patrol car on the main road passing by the side road she had pulled onto. Breathing a sigh of relief, Chantele figured she needed to find a deserted property somewhere that she could use as a hideout.

After a short while, the wind and rain ceased, and a beautiful rainbow appeared in the sky. She exclaimed to herself, "They say rainbows bring good luck, I surely deserve some for a change. Maybe good fortune might come my way. Here's hoping."

Her decision to avoid the main road because of the sighting of the patrol car took her further down the road she had turned onto. Unaware as to where the road led, she continued on, all the while looking for a safe haven. A few miles down the road she came across a fella trying to clean the debris out of the ditch in front of his house. The storm caused brush and small limbs to clog up the ditch, impeding the flow of the large amount of rainwater. She stopped, and after greeting him questioned, "Do you know of where I might be able to rent a room for several days. I have very few dollars, so it will have to be an inexpensive room rate. I was assaulted by two men, and escaped before they could take advantage of me. They stole my purse, which contained my ID along with most of the money I had. I feel so violated."

He answered, "I surely have no idea of any places around town that rent out rooms and we have no hotel nearby. I can let you stay here for a few days, if you are willing to help with cooking, wash dishes, and make up the beds in the morning. I have my farm to tend to, and I also do side work on another nearby farm. I could use your help if you plan to accept my offer and are willing to do what is needed here."

"I would love to do that for you. I am feeling much safer already."

Luck did smile on her. She found a room at a house in a very secluded part of the nearby county adjacent to Europa. She could also park her car in the barn to keep it clean and safe until she was able to get the much-needed repair work it required. It provided the perfect place, out of view of any police sighting, which was the real reason for storing it.

The lab work at school was completed, and Rose had returned home, happy, and safe in the security that it offered. The family was together again, and they could all somewhat relax about her safety.

Robbie was at the Colonel's farm and found it necessary to seek out Leon about some duties he had been neglecting. He noticed him going into the stable, and cried out to him, "Leon, hold up a minute, I would like to talk to you." Leon was not thrilled about this, and wondered what it was all about.

"Is it necessary? I'm in a hurry to get out of here. I have a lot going on at my place that requires my immediate attention."

"I am sure you do. It will only take a minute for me to share with you a concern we have about the job you are doing. The Colonel and I have been quite pleased with your work, but it seems that in the past week your quality has slipped. He is very particular about how the stalls are maintained, and he and I both agree that lately it is not being done properly. Do you have a problem keeping chores up at your farm, along with working here? We are concerned about the feeding of the horses, and it seems you are not maintaining the proper schedule. We discussed with you the importance of scheduling, along with feeding little and often."

"You know I want this job, and I feel that I'm doing everything just as explained to me at the start. You can count on me to do what is expected of me. I will pay more attention to the stalls, and make sure I get on the right feeding schedule. You can tell the Colonel that he can rely on it being done as you have spelled out."

Robbie was happy with Leon's reply. He smiled and told him, "I'm so glad that we have this understanding, and I am sure the Colonel will be happy regarding your agreement to do better. He does like you and will be glad to hear this from me."

As he departed, he started to think about what had just happened and he blurted aloud, "Why do I have to take his orders? I work for the Colonel, not him." Tomorrow, he intended to talk to his real boss and let him know that he did not like the arrangement.

When he arrived home, Chantele, who was awaiting his return, promptly questioned, "I expected you a lot earlier, what caused your delay?"

Leon replied, "You do know that I have an extra job, and it takes me every bit of a half an hour to get home?"

"I do. Who is it that you work for?"

"A Colonel living in Europa. I was being reprimanded and had to stay longer."

"I would have thought that he was a reasonable man and easy to deal with."

"Do you know him? It sounds as if you might."

"Right now, the question is, 'how do you get back in his good graces?'"

"Oh! I don't have a problem with the Colonel. It's this young upstart that supervises my work. He called me out today for not cleaning the stalls properly and got onto me about not maintaining a proper feeding schedule for the horses."

"Do you feel that you have fallen down on the job?"

"I may have cut corners a bit. I have been hurrying to get back here earlier as you have asked me to do."

"What is the name of this young guy you are talking about."

"I believe it's Robbie."

"Leon, what you need to do is tell the Colonel that you intend to do a good job, but you do not expect to be mistreated by somebody half your age."

He awakened the next day not sure that he was capable of carrying out her advice. Chantele sensed his reluctance and gave him a pep talk.

"You are a good worker, and do not deserve to be treated so badly. What does a young person like him know about things? I know you are the kind of person who always has and always will stand up for yourself. I am sure you know a whole lot more than he does. Let the Colonel know how you feel."

As he left, she took the opportunity to tell him how much he meant to her. "Leon, you are my hero, and I am beginning to fall in love with you." She kissed him on his cheek and gave him a long embrace.

She felt extremely confident that she had created a strong ally, and a very obliging one at that. He would be a big help in carrying out her plans.

He embarked for his meeting with the Colonel, fortified by her remarks and the feeling he got from her loving embrace. He felt he could do anything with her behind him. He had never felt about a woman as he felt about her.

Arriving at work he immediately went to the house and knocked on the door. The Colonel, an early riser, greeted him and welcomed him into the house.

"What can I do for you Leon?" the Colonel questioned.

"Sir, I need to discuss a situation that happened yesterday between Robbie and me."

"Tell me about it, Leon."

"Well, I was belittled by him, and he told me that I have not done anything right since being here. I would like to know why he gives me orders?"

"I will answer the question first. It is because he is truly knowledgeable, trustworthy, and very fair in his dealings. In regard to your conversations with him, I have a much different story as to what Robbie had said to you. He told you that he and I were quite pleased with your early efforts. He even commented as to how well you handled his assessment of your shortcomings and felt good about your response. He was extremely happy that you told him that you would rectify the problem, and to inform me not to worry because you would correct things."

"Colonel, do you believe a young man that makes up stories, or me?"

"Your conversation today makes it very hard for me to believe anything you might say."

"Are you saying that I no longer have a job with you?"

"I don't have to say it, your comments to me have taken care of that for you. Goodbye, Leon. I am sorry that it ended this way for you. Good luck with your farming. I hope all goes well for you."

Leon was dumbfounded. He did not expect things to go this way. He hung his head and walked out a defeated man.

Chapter 22:
A Foiled Plan

Rose looked out the window and noticed the mail carrier coming to the door with a large envelope. She hurried to greet him. He handed her the envelope and informed her it was for Rose Barrow. The mail had to be delivered to and signed by the addressee. She identified herself as the person he was seeking and signed for the parcel.

She excitedly opened the long-expected missive from the Office of the President of her college. Her expectations were high, and she was excited to receive the answer affecting her future at the college.

This information was intended to be presented to her in person while she was still conducting lab experiments after the end of the school year. It was not the message the President had hoped to deliver.

She read the letter aloud for her mother to hear.

> Dear Miss Barrow,
>
> It is with deep regret and suffering that I deliver the decision rendered by the College Board. Sadly, you will not be granted any financial help to cover next year's schooling expenses. They have decided in the favor of granting the meager funds available to twelve male seniors. This action allows for twelve, soon to graduate seniors, to enter the workforce and hopefully provide a much-needed impact in these uncertain times.
>
> I find the decision much to my dismay, but I have to agree with their logic. It would not benefit even you, if you were to receive what could be considered preferential treatment.

>   I, along with many others here, most
> certainly welcome your return to campus. I
> pray that the eventuality of that happening is
> made possible for you. Your absence would
> clearly be a significant loss to this
> institution, one which I personally regret.
>
>   I offer my best to you, and for great
> success in whatever you may be obligated to
> pursue.
>
> Sincerely,
>
>   President C. Donald Flavorson

Tears formed in her eyes as she absorbed the message and realized the consequences. She immediately resigned herself to the fact that she would not return to school but would try to find a job in order to help with the family finances.

The subject surfaced again as the family was at the table for the evening meal. Zack, as well as Elmo, were sorry about the decision, and were distressed they could not offer financial support for her to continue her education. They seemed to agree that her decision to find work had merit but wondered what else could be done.

Rose's personal cheerleader, and favorite former teacher heard of the news, and could not believe that even colleges were already feeling the effects of this spreading depression. He could not believe that this happened to somebody so deserving, and of such intelligence. He would try to see what he could do about the situation. He knew it would be a tough battle considering how bad the economy was. Earlier in the day, Mr. Spengler had received news of the owner of Spring's Mercantile committing suicide. He was so heavily in debt that the bank repossessed the business and all of his assets. It would not get better soon, making his quest to help Rose highly unlikely to bring the desired results.

The news fell upon the ears of an overly concerned and upset Colonel Burns. Within hours of hearing of Rose's plight, he was in conference with his friend, and former partner of his parents at the Brokerage Firm he now owned. He was in touch with the Admissions Office at Boston College. He spoke with former schoolmates, anybody he considered to be a mover and a shaker. He was going to get Rose enrolled and off to college one way or another. He was firm about one thing, if he could not arrange for a scholarship, he would foot the costs himself.

His fortitude and perseverance accomplished the task. He succeeded in securing a one-year scholarship and paid for her room and board. Should she not want to be apart from the family at such a far distance his prepayment was refundable in full.

Chantele, through her evil use of mental seduction, had completely manipulated Leon. She had him so enamored of her, that he would do anything she asked of him. Leon, or any of the others she had connected with were considered unworthy of her love. She reviled them, they were just pliable putty in her hands. She thought maybe Lonnie might be worthy. After all, he would soon be inheriting the business as well as a pretty nice home. She thought she might just go back after a while since his grandparents wouldn't live forever. She gave no thought to how she ignored them upon leaving and that she had not extended any sign of appreciation for the time she lived and dined there. She was an expert at leaving burning bridges behind her, in this case, the superstructure of the bridge had to be badly charred. Stealing fifty dollars from the station was not exactly an act that elicited a welcome back.

The Fourth of July came and went without any fanfare or hoopla of any sort. There was no Fair this year. There was little money to be had. What little was available could not be spent for frivolous purposes. Money was to be used for needs, not wants. The wants brought momentary delight; needs bought sustenance for continued life. These were hard times folks contended with.

Chantele, with the help of her compatriot, had devised a plan to seek retribution for all the ways she and he had been wronged. They were to travel to the house where Robbie lived and set fire to it while it was unoccupied. She would drive to the house from a back road that Leon had previously traveled with Robbie, while on a trip to pick up some feed. Under the cover of darkness, he would approach the house from the rear, and douse the wooden framed house with kerosene. He would throw a gasoline-soaked towel on that area, and retreat to where she was parked to make their getaway. She did not want for him to know there would be three women in the house. His last words to her were, "I do not want to hurt or maim anybody."

Rose's unknown guardian angel had been busy and had been informed by one of Rose's friends that Chantele was seen riding with a man on two occasions. Her appearance had drastically changed but her friend would bet that it was Chantele that she had seen. He followed up on the leads and felt confident that she was correct and had since kept a wary eye out for the pair. While out picking up a quilt from a friend's house, he thought he spotted them and intended to do surveillance to determine if he was right. His years on the police force served him well, and he proceeded with extreme caution. Following at a safe distance, he observed them turning on the back road leading to the Barrow property. To turn and follow would be a dead giveaway. He would approach quietly from the frontside, without headlights, and pull to the front of the long drive. He had no way of contacting the police and needed help from the folks in the house.

Proceeding cautiously up the drive to the house, he made it undetected to the front door. Tessie answered the door and was advised of the potential for a problem to develop. He told her not to panic, and to get to a phone and ask for immediate help. Mr. Alfred Rogers was making his way towards the back just as Leon ignited the towel to throw on the house. Tessie made the call for help and turned on the outside light.

Leon threw the ignited towel down on the ground, away from the building, and was heard to say, "Damned you, I thought you said nobody was going to be home." Al roared, "You are under arrest," and Leon threw his hands up in the air. He made no attempt to flee, and called out to his captor, "She is in the car on the back road."

Upon hearing that, Chantele sped away leaving another victim in her wake. The police arrived too late to catch her, and immediately sent out an APB in search of who they figured to be Chantele. Leon had never learned her name. She wanted to be called Honey.

Another scary night ended for the Barrow family. Rose questioned, "Will this growing nightmare ever end?"

The APB brought no success in finding the car that sped away. The great puppeteer had vanished once again. Meanwhile, Leon was booked on attempted murder, and intentional arson charges.

Appearing in Federal Court two weeks later, due to the testimony of Mr. Alfred Rogers, father of the young, imprisoned Mr. Rogers, Leon was acquitted of the arson charge. In his murder case, he was charged as an accessory to commit murder. He was sentenced to eight years for his involvement.

Chapter 23:
Wartime Service

Rose was requested to meet with Colonel Burns and rode along with Robbie who was going there to attend to needed chores. She was welcomed into the house and the Colonel expressed his concern over the recent chain of events. He went on to share, "It will not be long before she is behind bars where she belongs. You are a brave woman and of strong faith. Keep believing that this will soon come to pass.

I have heard of the depressing news regarding the loss of your scholarship, and I have taken steps to remedy your situation. The arrangements have been made for you to have an expense-free education at Boston College. All that remains is for you to say yes."

Rose was speechless and remained that way for what seemed an eternity. She composed herself, and finally asked, "How could that be possible? I haven't made attempts for that to happen."

"I know that, Rose. What is important at this time is for you to determine if that is what you want, and if you will accept the offer. It would be such a waste of the vast talent that you have been blessed with, should you not accept. It would please me, your parents, siblings, and many others if you were to do so. Please do not deprive people of all that you have to offer and are capable of delivering."

Rose was brought to tears at hearing the news of this generous offer and cried out, "I am pleased and honored to do so. I will never be able to repay you for your kindness and cannot thank you enough for caring. Excuse my tears. They are of joy for the love and kindness you have showered our family with."

Time continued to slip away. Camelia graduated from High School, and the Colonel made arrangements for her to also attend Boston College. She and Rose would be roommates for two years while she pursued her degree in Education. Robbie would be finishing his last year in High School. The Colonel advocated for Robbie to pursue a degree in Veterinary Medicine, and Robbie was inclined to do so.

While rooming together Camelia intercepted a considerable number of threatening messages meant for Rose. She forwarded them to the Security Officer, who assured her that everything would be done to prevent harm from coming to her sister. Keeping the messages away from Rose gave her some peace of mind and allowed her to concentrate on her studies.

Tessie continued with her position in the cafeteria at school. It seemed that her ongoing employment would not be interrupted. Zack and Elmo had done well with the sale of their farm crops, and again were going to increase the space to grow more soybeans.

Robbie was doing well in school, growing into manhood, and likewise in stature. Colonel Burns was extremely proud of his protégé and had grown very fond of him. The relationship was good medicine for both of them. He treated him like his own son and there were many times that the Colonel found himself wishing he were.

Chantele had fallen off the face of the Earth. The searches did not result in securing any information that proved to be helpful in finding her. They knew that she existed because the hateful and frightening notes continued to surface. How she managed to deliver the notes without being apprehended bewildered law enforcement officials. They believed she had connected with another male puppet.

The sale of the soybeans resulted in bringing in some much-needed cash. Zack and Elmo decided to again increase the plot and grow more beans. It was a sound decision but resulted in more concerns for the family. While clearing the space needed, Elmo was injured. The plow he was pulling with the tractor got snagged on a large root. Due to the light weight of the engine, the tractor's front end raised and fell backwards on top of Elmo. He was fortunate that the steering column prevented the full weight of the machine from coming down on him.

Zack took him to see Dr. Morgan to ensure he did not suffer from any internal injuries. The doctor told Zack, "All is well, and the burns caused from the hot engine are superficial and should heal in a short time. It is a good thing that your father-in-law is so ornery. He will be all right with a lot of pampering. He likes that."

Elmo threw a barb at the doctor, "Zack you better check the bill. He will probably charge you for the sarcastic advice he hands out."

Rose graduated with a bachelor's degree in biology and received the distinction of Summa Cum Laude. She had a decision to make since she decided not to continue her original plan to become a nurse. She ultimately decided on the discipline she would pursue in the next phase of her education, and her benefactor for all these years was immensely proud of her choice. Her Scholarship award had been extended to cover tuition as well as room and board costs for her extended studies.

Tessie hosted a graduation party for Rose, with special guests, Colonel Burns, and former teacher, Mr. Spengler, in attendance. It was a day to celebrate her achievements thus far, in her short and disrupted life. The pride felt for her, coming from all in attendance, filled the room, and meant so much to a lovely young lady. She thanked everyone and cited what each individual had contributed to her success in life.

Rose was preparing for her next step in her scholastic life, just as several young men were attending a party hosted for them. They would be leaving for the state of Oregon while in the employment of the newly formed Works Progress Administration. President Franklin D. Roosevelt created the program in June of 1935 in order to lift the country out of the Great Depression. The purpose was to provide for necessary infrastructure improvements, and to reduce the growing unemployment numbers. Elmo and Zack attended the event and were responsible for initiating a collection to be given to the two young lads. Not a single person in attendance failed to find a way to donate to the cause.

The depression lingered on, and a vast part of Europe felt the terror that resulted from the blitzkrieg that was being rained on them by the attacking German forces. It began with the attack on Poland in September of 1939 by Nazi Germany, the Slovak Republic, and the Soviet Union. This action marked the start of World War ll.

While the conflict waged in Europe, the folks in the little town of Europa wondered what effect that war would have on them. Life went on, but the question lingered and captured their fearful attention.

Rose had completed her education and was working in the field for which she had prepared. Camelia taught at the local Elementary School, and Robbie was engaged in Veterinary practice while still operating his stud service. Tessie was retired. She, and along with Zack and Elmo, devoted all their attention to the needs of Happy Acres Farm.

The question that plagued the townsfolk was answered on December 7, 1941. It was the morning a sneak attack on the American Naval Base at Pearl Harbor Honolulu, Hawaii was perpetrated by Imperial Japanese Forces. On that day, 2403 American lives were lost. The Pacific Fleet lay in ruins. The next day, December 8, 1941, our President delivered his "Day of Infamy Speech" and declared war on Japan. In December of 1941, the United States entered into the fighting of World War ll. In the early stages of the war, the U.S. supplied the European Countries with war supplies through the Lend Lease Act.

The first peacetime draft in U.S. history was put in effect on September 16, 1940. Men between 21 and 35 years of age were required to register for the draft. Following the attack on Pearl Harbor, the age requirement became 21 to 64.

Rose enlisted into the service of the U.S. Army on February 2, 1942, at the rank of Captain. Robbie attempted to join but was given a deferment due to his profession. The Army needed beef pork and chickens to feed the troops, and the animals needed Veterinarians to keep them healthy.

The Works Progress Program ended in 1943, due to the increased employment necessary to serve the war effort. In the time it was in effect 8.5 million people were employed.

Victory in Europe was declared on May 7, 1945, and the end to hostilities with Japan came on September 2, 1945. Rose was discharged in April of 1947 at the rank of Colonel. The army was downsizing, and her specialty was being filled by Regular Army Officers who had more time in service. A fond farewell was held to honor the outgoing head of Neurosurgery at Walter Reed Army Medical Center, and to welcome her new replacement. He was a doctor whom she chose as an assisting surgeon on numerous occasions. She felt good about the decision and was happy to have had the privilege to serve her country.

Chapter 24:
Winter Woes

With the war behind them, everybody was about the business of returning to a normal life. Rose was back at the position she filled prior to her enlistment. Life was much better now. The increased production found the country enjoying a bustling economy. People were back to work and rationing of meat, sugar, gas, tires, and other essential items was no longer necessary.

It was late springtime, and the business at Happy Acres Farm became very brisk. The worries about being able to pay the bills in order to keep the business from going into foreclosure was no longer a concern. The family was doing well health-wise and financially. Camelia loved her new position as Superintendent of Schools for Webster County, and Robbie had become the go-to Veterinarian throughout the entire area.

Sad news traveled fast. Zack received a disturbing call regarding the passing of the Colonel. He left this world at the young age of sixty-six, seventeen years after arriving in Europa. His breathing problems resurfaced and ultimately led to his demise. Dr. Morgan performed the autopsy and specified that complications resulting from a wound received in battle impaired his breathing.

He had no living family members and being an orderly person, had prepared for this eventuality. A letter, to be opened upon his passing, was placed in the hands of Dr. Morgan many years ago. His wishes were to be buried in the Church Graveyard, and to have a Military Honor Guard at the grave site. An additional wish was to have Rose Barrow, also a Colonel, deliver the Eulogy.

It was a beautiful day, fitting for a man of his distinction. The church was incapable of holding all the mourners present to pay tribute to a special man. The minister, Caleb Short, did all he could to accommodate the throng that gathered for the service. Extra chairs were placed outside the church doors to be used by the handicapped and the elderly. When the service began, it was estimated that more than two hundred were in attendance, with more people making their way.

The ceremony was beautifully performed, and the choir's rendition of "Amazing Grace" brought tears to the eyes of most of the crowd. After delivering her inspirational and eloquent Eulogy, Rose asked the attendees to do one special act of kindness in honor of a kind, giving, honest, and caring war hero. She then assembled the girls that performed at the Fair where Colonel Burns was the principal speaker. She implored everyone, "I pray that each and every one will join in the singing of 'America the Beautiful' and 'God Bless America.'" The renditions were well done and could be heard almost a mile away as the melodious voices joyfully joined in to honor their hero.

The bugler rendered "Taps" to an adoring and sorrowful group of tearful mourners, ending the Celebration of Life for Colonel Robert Burns. As the crowd departed, there were many conversations praising the man for the good that he offered to them. One could hear words of gratitude coming from many people he knew. They recognized the help he unselfishly offered for one cause or another.

Rose was mentally and physically exhausted and could not spend any more time with the family. It was necessary for her to return to the obligations facing her back home.

Spring turned into fall and was soon to be greeted by the vicissitudes of an unforgiving winter. The weather in the eastern part of the country was a threat to life and limb. Traffic was coming to a standstill, as the snowfall became heavier. At the

Boston General Hospital, a fatigued doctor was just finishing a lengthy operation on a young child with a severe brain injury caused by a sledding accident.

The lonely doctor would be able to visit with family for Christmas because of a change made with another doctor who wanted to be off on New Year's Eve. The change suited both of them. One wanted to be with family, the other wanted to celebrate with friends.

On this wintry night of New Year's Eve, the doctor rested in the lounge, waiting for the next emergency case to come in that required the doctor's surgical acumen. Thankfully, the activity waned, and it was relatively quiet and peaceful for some time.

Sirens blared everywhere as police, fire, and emergency vehicles were being dispatched in response to varying calls for help. Soon the sirens would be headed to the aid of a woman who had been traveling at too high of speeds for the prevailing road conditions. Upon their arrival on the scene, the officers were immediately aware that the person was intoxicated and was in dire need of immediate medical attention if she were to survive.

She was transported to the nearest hospital in order to ensure her survival. The emergency doors flung open as the ambulance drivers carted the lifeless person into the emergency room. Her head was so severely damaged that her facial features were indistinguishable. The severity of the injuries she sustained required immediate attention from highly skilled hands.

A nurse came into the lounge to wake a tired, overworked doctor in order to prepare for the operation. The doctor, in somewhat of a fog, went about making the necessary preparations. Upon entering the O.R., she was suddenly overcome by a strange feeling. It was unlike any feeling ever experienced, though she had been in numerous similar situations. It caused a competent and practiced surgeon to pause and question if there was a connection between her and the patient.

The assisting nurse handed the chart to the doctor, who noticed the patient was recognized as Jane Doe. They had no identification of who she might be. The doctor questioned herself. *Am I about to perform a lifesaving operation on who I think this is?* She was not sure that she should go ahead with the operation or call in another specialist to perform the procedure. The answer quickly came into her mind. She had taken the Hippocratic Oath and would do it to the best of her ability.

After six long hours, a preeminent neurosurgeon, Dr. Rose Barrow Spicer, skillfully performed a miraculous lifesaving surgery. Her patient, who was unrecognizable as well as unidentifiable, was in the ICU and expected to make it. The operating staff was in complete awe of the precision exhibited by the highly skilled surgeon.

While in recovery and still under the effects of the anesthesia, Jane Doe repeatedly muttered two unintelligible words. Two hours later, the patient had recovered from the effects of the anesthesia and was able to give her full name. The nurses in the ICU seemed to think she may have been repeating the name of Rose Barrow but were not really sure that was what they were hearing. One asked the other, "How could she possibly be calling out the doctor's name when she had no way of knowing who her doctor was."

The two moved out of range of the patient's hearing and decided one of them would call out the name they thought they heard. The other would observe closely to see if there was any noticeable reaction from the patient. While doing so it became evident that they had stumbled on something.

The decision was made to directly question her to determine if she was really calling out the name Rose Barrow. The patient in her weakened state nodded affirmatively and began to sob. They did not expect this reaction and became concerned they may have possibly jeopardized her well-being. A mild sedative was administered to prevent any type of relapse they may have caused from the questioning.

When she had sufficiently recovered, Chantele requested to see the surgeon who performed the surgery that had saved her life.

Dr. Barrow Spicer entered her room, fully believing that it was Chantele who had been brought in for the emergency surgery that night. Her belief was confirmed as soon as she entered her room, as Chantele tearfully confessed, "Rose, I am sure by now you know who I am. I want to tell you that I am sorry for causing you so much worry and fear of harm all these years. I especially want to inform you that I am extremely grateful that you saved my life. Even in my sedated state, I felt that you were the doctor performing the surgery."

Rose responded, "I had a strange feeling you were the unfortunate emergency patient, and I am glad you are confirming the fact now. I am sorry about your terrible accident, and pleased I was able to help you in your distress. I forgive you for your actions, and passionately believe that you are repentant for what you have done. I am sorry that you will be moved from here to the prison when sufficiently recovered. There are guards stationed outside your door to prevent your escape, should you attempt to do so."

She conceded, "I know I have done wrong, and I accept the fact that I am deserving of whatever sentence is imposed on me. I wish that my life would have been lived differently."

The day after the accident, the headlines in the Boston Herald read:
PREEMINENT NEUROSURGEON SAVES LIFE OF HER INTENDED KILLER.

Three weeks later the headlines were:
ASPIRING MURDERER OF FAMED SURGEON TO STAND TRIAL.

Several months later, the District Attorney argued for the Death Penalty since Chantele's two attempts were premeditated. The decision of the Jury found her guilty on both counts of Attempted Murder. The sentence imposed was Life Imprisonment with no parole. As with most court decisions there were detractors of the final decision.

Chapter 25:
Lives Well Lived

Years after performing the lifesaving operation, Rose sat in her study and ruminated about the fortunes of her life. She focused on the role Colonel Burns had played in their life and dwelled on the fact that he was responsible for the Barrow children's education.

She thought of his kind, benevolent and charitable giving, how upon his death he willed his property in Europa to Robbie, Camelia, and her, and how his business holdings in Boston were divided between his faithful employees, and a vast portion to Boston College.

She reflected on the years of threatening notes that kept her in constant fear for her own safety and that of her family. She thought about the misfortunes of Chantele, and of the prison life she was now serving.

Rose was eternally grateful that her mother and father in their early seventies were still living at the old farmstead. Grandpa, who lived a great life, passed on some seven years earlier. Camelia, the County School Superintendent, and her family happily live in the Colonel's former home. All was well in Europa, but the Barrow family was missing Robbie.

She concentrated her thoughts on brother Robbie, and how proud she was of his tremendous accomplishments. She reflected on his being the owner of the American Riding Academy in the picturesque horse country of Warrenton, Virginia. He, in the spirit of his benefactor, Colonel Burns, hired Maximillian Brunner as Headmaster. And in order to help out another of Chantele's pawns and victims, had hired Leon Sparks as the Stablemaster. His Academy was the premier Equine Center in all of the country.

She envisioned Sparky and Rusty, occupying spacious stalls befitting of their contributions that allowed for the success of his operations.

Her reverie was interrupted by her husband, Denny Spicer, renown Horticulturist, and developer of seven varieties of roses. He told her, "Rose dear, dinner is served, and the children are awaiting your much desired company."

She and her husband were the proud parents of two children, Robert, and Rosealee. Both attended Mississippi State U., originally named Agricultural and Mechanical College of Mississippi, where Rose and Denny first met. They were on furlough from the Army for two weeks, prior to reassignment.

Storm clouds had gathered once again. War was being waged on the Asian continent between North and South Korea. An unprovoked invasion by North Korea led to the United States involvement. The motivation was to protect a non-communist country from takeover by a communist regime.

A saddened, and proud mother offered her advice to her soldier children as they were about to depart. "Rosealee and Robert, you may be given an assignment to an area where your lives may be in danger. You have been well trained to be ready for this eventuality. Put what you have been taught to work for you."

"I recently read a quote from the author John A. Shedd. I quote his words, 'A ship at harbor is safe, but that's not what ships were built for.' A soldier takes an oath to protect his country, you two are soldiers, live by your oath. Be wise and cautious, keep your faith, and return to us after you have faithfully performed your sworn duty. Your father and I love you very much."

"I will offer, there are no good-byes, so long for now, until we meet again. God bless and keep you both, and God bless America, our citizens, and all our troops."

THE END

Seeking forgiveness from someone you offended or reconnecting with someone who wronged you are keys to securing eternal happiness. Sleep is much more restful after doing so.

About The Author

John Stanczak is an aspiring author who has now finished his fourth published work. He was born in northern Illinois in 1930, the era of the Great Depression. He served in the United States Army from 1951 through 1954 during the Korean War. He went on to become a successful entrepreneur before retiring at the age of eighty-one. He currently resides in Brentwood, Tennessee.

This aspiring author has now finished his fourth published work in his late years of life. His latest offering, *America, of Thee I Sing*, began as a sequel to a previously published children's book. It was intended to relate further adventures of Buzzy the Bee, while introducing Rufus the dog, a friend to Ruckus the horse. His failure to do so inevitably resulted in the creation of this mystery novel. It proved to be an exhilarating experience and may lead to another story incorporating characters from both of the books. If it were to become a reality, it will certainly be his last endeavor. At the soon to be age of ninety-three, the task becomes a bit more taxing.

Visit www.johnrstanczak.com for more information.

Also by John R. Stanczak

The Story of the Stanczak Brothers Baseball Team: Baseball's All Brothers World Champions

Musings... An Old Man's Recollections of Life's Events

The Adventures of Buzzy the Bee & His Friends

Cover Image: AZ Imaging via Getty Images

Printed in the USA
CPSIA information can be obtained
at www.ICGtesting.com
LVHW030830220124
769165LV00014B/1057

9 798218 332488